D1112544

Wonka

Books by Roald Dahl

The BFG

Billy and the Minpins

Boy: Tales of Childhood

Charlie and the Chocolate Factory

Charlie and the Great Glass Elevator

Danny the Champion of the World

Dirty Beasts

The Enormous Crocodile

Esio Trot

Fantastic Mr. Fox

George's Marvelous Medicine

The Giraffe and the Pelly and Me

Going Solo

James and the Giant Peach

The Magic Finger

Matilda

The Missing Golden Ticket and Other Splendiferous Secrets

Revolting Rhymes

The Twits

The Vicar of Nibbleswicke

The Witches

The Wonderful Story of Henry Sugar and Six More

INSPIRED BY
ROALD DAHL'S
CHARLIE AND THE CHOCOLATE FACTORY

Written by **SIBÉAL POUNDER**
Based on the screenplay by **SIMON FARNABY** & **PAUL KING**
Story by **PAUL KING**

VIKING

VIKING

An imprint of Penguin Random House LLC, New York

First published in the United Kingdom by Penguin Books UK, 2023
First published in the United States of America by Viking,
an imprint of Penguin Random House LLC, 2023

Visit us online at PenguinRandomHouse.com.

Library of Congress Cataloging-in-Publication Data is available.

ISBN 9780593528686 (hardcover)

ISBN 9780593690758 (international edition)

ScoutAutomatedPrintCode

Printed in the United States of America

LSCC

Design by Dynamo Limited

Text set in Bembo MT Pro

HOW WILLY BECAME WONKA
THE JOURNEY OF AN
INCREDIBLE STORY

Willy Wonka—Roald Dahl's marvelous chocolate inventor from his book *Charlie and the Chocolate Factory*—inspired the story behind the major motion picture *Wonka*. Paul King drew from the classic book to create this story, which he co-wrote for the screen with Simon Farnaby, of how the world's greatest inventor, magician, and chocolate-maker becomes the Willy Wonka we know today. It has been adapted and brought to the page by bestselling children's author Sibéal Pounder—an expert in crafting stories full of irreverent humor, charismatic characters, and magic for young readers.

Roald Dahl was the author of the much-loved *Charlie and the Chocolate Factory*, among many other brilliant stories. It is the world and characters of *Charlie and the Chocolate Factory*, and in particular the character of Willy Wonka, that inspired this story of how Willy became Wonka.

Roald Dahl was a spy, ace fighter pilot, chocolate historian, and medical inventor. In addition to writing *Charlie and the Chocolate Factory*, he was the author of *Matilda*, *The BFG*, *Fantastic Mr. Fox*, and many more.

Paul King is a lifelong fan of *Charlie and the Chocolate Factory*, and for his movie *Wonka*, he decided he wanted to tell the story of the events before the book takes place. He created the adventure you hold in your hands and partnered up with Simon Farnaby to write the screenplay for the film, which stars Timothée Chalamet as Willy Wonka.

Paul King is a BAFTA-nominated writer/director who works in both film and television. In 2009, King wrote and directed his first feature film, *Bunny and the Bull*, starring Simon Farnaby and Edward Hogg. King directed all three series of *The Mighty Boosh*, earning him a BAFTA nomination for Best New Director in 2005. The BBC comedy aired in the US on Adult Swim. His most recent work for the small screen includes directing and executive producing episodes of the 2020 Netflix series *Space Force*, starring Steve Carell.

King then went on to co-write and direct *Paddington* in 2014, a film which received both critical and commercial success worldwide, including BAFTA nominations for Best Adapted Screenplay and Best British Film. King next co-wrote and directed *Paddington 2*, released by Warner Bros. Pictures in 2017 to great critical acclaim. Both Paddington movies were co-written with Simon Farnaby.

Simon Farnaby co-scripted *Wonka*, alongside Paul King, and appears in an on-screen role. He is an actor and writer whose starring film credits include *Burke & Hare* (directed by John Landis, 2010); *Your Highness* (directed by David Gordon Green, 2011); *Bill* (directed by Richard Bracewell, 2015), for BBC Films, loosely based on the early life of William Shakespeare; and *Bunny and the Bull* (directed by Paul King, 2009), for Film4. He also appeared in writer/director King's critically acclaimed BAFTA-nominated hit *Paddington* and reprised his role for the equally acclaimed sequel, *Paddington 2*, which he co-wrote with King, receiving two BAFTA nominations himself.

Sibéal Pounder, bestselling children's author, has brought this story to the page, adapting it from the screenplay with extraordinary skill.

She is the author of the bestselling Witch Wars and Bad Mermaids series of books, *Neon's Secret Universe*, and the Christmas tale *Tinsel*. Her debut, *Witch Wars*, was shortlisted for the Sainsbury's Children's Book Award and the Waterstones Children's Book Prize. The Bad Mermaids series was a World Book Day title and a *Sunday Times* bestseller. Before becoming a full-time author, Pounder worked for the *Financial Times*.

CONTENTS

HERE COMES WONKA

S ome children are born to be chocolate makers. This was certainly true of Willy Wonka.

Yet, for a long time, no one would've thought it. For starters, he almost never ate chocolate. In fact, he ate only *one bar* a year.

One day, he would grow up to live in the world's **BIGGEST** chocolate factory, but as a young boy, Willy Wonka lived on the world's smallest boat. It was an old narrow boat, with a tiller painted in multicolored stripes and a cozy cabin with handsewn curtains. Inside there was just a single bed with a soft knitted blanket (where Willy slept), an armchair (where his mother slept), a stove, and a kitchen filled with broken cupboards and a worm-eaten dining table. The woodworms ate more at that table than the Wonkas ever did.

Everything about the beginning of this story is **SMALL**—the small boy, the small quantity of chocolate, the small boat, and the small family who lived aboard it. Willy Wonka's family was almost as small as a family could be. There was Willy, of course, and his mother.

They moored their small boat on a quiet **STRETCH** of the river, and, as not many people from town ventured there, they often had the lush riverbank all to themselves. It was one of Willy's favorite places. There was tall grass for lazing in, sprinkled with buttercups and rhododendrons flowering in colors of pink and mauve and red. Willy's favorite part was the

GIGANTIC willow tree, with its thick branches that swooped low over the boat before dipping into the river. He thought of the tree as another member of the family—a twiggy old protector of their small but grand life.

Not many people would see their life as *grand*, of course, but Willy Wonka did. He could see what others couldn't because he had the most wonderful imagination. Willy's imagination would one day become as famous as his chocolate, but before it belonged to the world, it was small and new and belonged only to him. His mother was the one who nurtured it, letting it grow wild, so it could spin off into places no imagination had been before.

And then there was the chocolate. The one bar. It wasn't much, but it was enough, because it was the best bar in the world.

His mother would make it for his birthday, and as the special day approached, he would feel the excitement **BUBBLING** up in him until he thought he might burst.

The chocolate-making ritual was always the same: his mother would tip a bag of cocoa beans onto the table and carefully count them out. He'd watch her pluck them from the table, one by one, and his mouth would begin to water. It took her all year to save up enough money to buy the right amount for one bar, and he could tell she was as excited about making it for him as he was about eating it.

When the counting stage was finished, she'd throw the beans in a pot and begin crushing and whipping and stirring, and the whole room would be engulfed in a chocolaty steam. It was so **THICK** and delicious, it felt like being swept up in the most scrumptious cloud. Oh, how he loved to watch her stir the thick, bubbling mixture!

As his mother made magic, Willy took long deep sniffs of the rich, heavy smell and knew there would be no adventure in the world that he loved more than watching his mama make chocolate.

Soon, the delicious bar of chocolate would be waiting for him on the table, and he'd spend the rest of the day walking around with a melted-chocolate mustache and a big grin.

It was like that every year, and it was perfect.

"You know, Mama," he said one year as they **HUDDLED** around the table making chocolate, "I bet you make the best chocolate in the whole world. I'd taste all the chocolate that ever existed just to prove it!"

"Do you know where they say the very best chocolate in the world comes from?" she replied, looking around as if she was readying to tell a great secret. "The Galeries Gourmet. That's where the finest chocolate makers have their shops."

"Theirs can't be better than yours, Mama," Willy said. "It's impossible!"

She smiled. "Well, as it so happens, I do have a little secret that even those fancy pants don't know."

"What is it?" Willy asked, edging closer. He wanted to know the secret more than he'd ever wanted to know anything in his whole life.

"I'll tell you one day," she said. "Now, while the chocolate sets, would you like to open your present?"

"We should go, Mama!" he cried suddenly, making her jump.

"Where's that, then?"

"To the Galeries Gourmet!" he said, practically bouncing on the spot. "We could start a shop!"

She raised a curious eyebrow. "What? *Us?*"

"Yes! With our name above the door and everything. **WONKA!** Everyone in the world would want our chocolate. Think how happy we could make people!"

His mother brushed some chocolate dust from her apron and smiled. "Oh, I can see it now. A fine shop, tables piled high with chocolate!"

Willy's eyes grew wide as the place materialized in his mind. "And the tables would be *made* of chocolate! The whole *shop* would be *made* of CHOCOLATE!"

His mother beamed. "What a wonderful dream, Willy."

He slumped. "Is that all it is? Just a dream?"

"Hey, now," she said. "Every good thing in this world started with a dream. So you hold on to yours. And when you do share your chocolate with the world, I'll be right there beside you."

"You promise?" he whispered.

"I pinkie promise," she said with a smile. "And that's the most solemn vow there is." Then she took a piece of paper, which she'd set aside to wrap the chocolate, and wrote **WONKA** across it, adding a swish and a swirl to the *W* and carefully coloring it in.

Once she'd finished, she handed Willy something wrapped in old newspaper. "Your present," she said. "The magician in town was selling it. Did me a good deal."

Willy beamed and began ripping the package open, his fingers working fast to tear the inky paper.

Inside, he found a new coat. He pulled it on; his hands barely went past the elbows.

"You'll grow into it," his mother said. "One day you will—and, oh, the adventures you'll have in it!"

The coat came with a **TALL** hat. Slowly he placed it on his head and rose to his feet.

His mother handed him his chocolate, small

and still warm, and he cradled it in his hands like the most precious prize.

"Mustn't forget the most **DELICIOUS** bit," she said with a wink.

He beamed at her, and then he slipped the bar into his pocket.

There he was.

Willy Wonka, in his plum-colored tailcoat and fine top hat.

CHAPTER ONE

CITY OF DREAMS

SEVEN YEARS LATER

Willy stood on the deck of an old fishing ship, cloaked in mist and smiling brightly. All around him, the weather-worn crew was busying themselves on deck, and young Mr. Wonka couldn't have looked more out of place in his bright green waistcoat and multicolored scarf.

"Seven years I've been at sea," he said to a nearby fisherman, who was **SCRUBBING** a crate (and barely listening). "But now it's time for a new adventure! My next stop is almost upon us."

"Oh, really?" the fisherman said. Everyone on board had grown quite used to Willy's strange tales and flights of fancy by now.

"Every minute the waves lap me closer to my dreams," Willy said grandly.

"Where's that, then?" the fisherman asked.

Willy grinned and pointed to the horizon. There, glinting brightly in the winter sun, was the city he had pinned all his hopes on. It looked even more marvelous than he had imagined, sprawling and grand and—he took a big sniff—the *smell* was the best part of all! The whole place, even from afar, smelled of chocolate! Oh, it was **HEAVENLY** . . . even when mingled with the scent of barrels full of fish.

He pulled a small, old chocolate bar from his pocket. The makeshift wrapper was faded now, but his mother's writing still remained. He traced his fingers over the swirly letters.

A harbor bell sounded in the distance.

"LAND AHOY!" Willy cried.

"They won't know what's hit 'em, Mr. Wonka," the fisherman said with a chuckle, and he headed off to ready the boat to dock. Willy took one last great big sniff of chocolaty air before trotting inside to the engine room. There he scooped up his trusty plum-colored tailcoat and top hat, a battered case, and a fine item he had acquired on his travels—a long cane with a sparkling gold top. He was **GIDDY** with anticipation as he absentmindedly put his hat on, took it off, tucked it under his arm, then lifted his cane and put it over his shoulder before putting it down again. It was as if the **EXCITEMENT** had so overwhelmed him that he'd forgotten where a hat went and how to carry a cane.

A polite cough made him jump and he spun on

his heel to see the kindly eyes of the ship's captain staring back at him. He was a tall man with a beard as long as his years at sea (which is as long as it takes hair to grow to your knees). "Here," the captain said, holding out a weathered fist and opening it to reveal a bag of coins.

Willy peeked inside. *"Twelve silver sovereigns?"* he cried in amazement. It was more money than he had ever held in his hand before and he thought he might collapse under the sheer weight of such a **GENEROUS** lump sum.

"Your wages, plus a little extra for all those delicious chocolates you made for us," the captain said. "We all put in as much as we could, and it's not much—not for the big city—but I hope it'll start you off right. Good luck to you, lad."

The boat **JOLTED** and groaned as they made contact with the dock and Willy pulled his top hat down firmly on his head.

"Thank you, Captain," he said, the nerves now rising in him like a fast tide.

A crate was being craned out of the hold and Willy jumped onto it and up he went, leaving the amused captain in his wake.

"You could've used the gangplank!" a fisherman holding a gangplank shouted as Willy shot up past him. "If you'd given me a second . . ."

"I haven't a second to lose!" Willy called down to him. He paused as the crane winched the crate higher and swung it around the dock, then he spread his arms wide and cried, "TODAY IS THE DAY! THE DAY THE WORLD MEETS MY CHOCOLATE!"

Instantly, someone shouted, "Is there a person on that crate?!" There was a screech of metal and the crane came to an abrupt halt. The crane's operator stuck his head out of the control cabin and locked eyes with Willy.

"YOU CAN'T SIT ON A CRANE!" he cried incredulously. "GET OFF!"

"If you insist, sir," Willy said, and then much to the **ASTONISHMENT** of the crowd watching on the dock, he dived right off it—headfirst! There was a collective holding of breath as Willy somersaulted down to the sound of nothing but the wind and his own thumping heartbeat. It may have looked impressive, but Willy hadn't really thought it through and was wide-eyed with fear as his face led the way to the pavement. Luckily, there was a truck passing at just the right time to catch him—otherwise this story would be very short indeed.

"ON TO MY DREAMS!" Willy cheered as he flipped and landed perfectly upright on the roof of the truck. It trundled off toward the town, leaving a crowd of gaping jaws behind him.

The truck sped over a grand stone bridge dotted

with warming lanterns, and all the way into the heart of the city . . . which was better than anything Willy Wonka had imagined. It was dusted like a doughnut in fresh snow and perfect in every way. There were intriguing cobblestone alleys peppered with shops painted in the **PRETTIEST** of blues and pinks and purples that went left and right and right and left, just like a rabbit warren. And the smell! The closer they got to the center of town, the more it intensified, and Willy couldn't help but sigh with **DELIGHT**. The truck passed through the town square and he took his chance, grabbing hold of a lamppost and swinging round as he watched the vehicle speed off, leaving nothing but air beneath his feet. The place was so packed to bursting that not a single soul had spotted him high up on the lamppost, and he slid down, landing among a sea of potential customers.

He'd never been somewhere so busy or so

loud. He found himself trying to gulp it all in, his eyes darting left, right, up, and down and every angle in between all at once! On one side of the square was an imposing cathedral, with impossibly tall oak doors and a roof so high it looked like it might be attached to heaven. There were shops on every corner, with windows crammed with perfumes and shoes and books and paints, and food carts rolled back and forth, nearly knocking him sideways. The square was lined with decadent columns and the center was marked with an ornate fountain frozen solid in the cold. It twinkled in the sunlight like it was filled with stars pulled from the sky.

The whole place was impossibly **BEAUTI-FUL**. But the most beautiful building of all was the Galeries Gourmet.

Willy stopped when he caught it in his sights— its domes glinting, its doors a shimmering, inviting blue, its smell nothing but pure chocolate.

"Wow," he whispered as he stared his dream in the face. He felt light and tingly and smiled a dozy smile. He'd waited his whole life to see it, and, finally, here he—

"RESTAURANT MAP, SIR?" a man shouted in his ear, shattering his thoughts.

Willy handed the man a sovereign, and in turn the man gave him a map.

"This will show you the **BEST** restaurants, sir," the man said. Noticing Willy's stare was still fixed on the Galeries Gourmet, he added, "You can't only eat chocolate, after all!"

"Oh, of course not!" Willy agreed. "You must also have *sweets*."

He unfolded the map to give it a quick look, but as he did so, he spotted someone crouching at his feet. A young boy was waving a rag about and polishing his shoes!

"Er, excuse me," Willy said.

"Yes, yes, almost finished!" the boy replied. He took out a big buffing pad and began running it over the toes. "Right, done," he said, and held out a hand for payment.

Willy was racking his brains, trying to remember if in all the **EXCITEMENT** he had arranged to have his shoes cleaned. He handed the boy one of his sovereigns in any case and counted the ones that remained.

"Oh dear, I'm already down to ten sovereigns," he said.

At that moment, a fruit cart trundled past, and Willy plucked a pumpkin from it and gave it a good sniff. But before he had a chance to put it back, a cyclist shot past, clipping his ankles, and the pumpkin slipped from his grasp and splatted on his boots!

The fruit seller loomed over him, eyeing the

pile of mulch on the pavement. "That's three sovereigns, mate."

"Three? That's a rather extreme price for a vegetable," Willy said with a charming smile.

The seller was gravely serious.

"You broke my pumpkin, you pay for it," she snapped, making Willy jump so suddenly, the three sovereigns leaped from his hand and into the OUTSTRETCHED palm of the seller.

"Pleasure doing business with you," she said.

Willy began counting his remaining coins. "I've got five, six, sev—" He felt a prod on his shoe. The shoeshine boy was back again!

He wiped the pumpkin sludge off and held out a hand for payment.

". . . six silver sovereigns," Willy groaned as he gave the boy another coin, and then made for the Galeries Gourmet.

"Brush your coat, sir?" the shoeshine boy asked as he hurried after him.

Willy quickened his pace. "No, thank you."

The boy darted in front of him and held up a chipped old bottle. "Cologne?"

"Absolutely not—I only fragrance myself with chocolate," Willy said, leaving the boy blinking with confusion behind him.

Porters threw open the doors and announced grandly, "Welcome, sir, to the Galeries Gourmet." At this point, the sweetest, most delicious aroma flooded the street, and Willy was almost knocked sideways by the **SCRUMPTIOUSNESS** of it all. He stood staring at what lay beyond. It wasn't just an arcade full of shops to him—it was his dreams piled high in stone and glass. He closed his eyes and touched the pocket where he kept his mother's bar of chocolate.

"Here we go, Mama," he whispered, and with a brave step, he entered.

Inside, the place had the **AROMA** of dreams and chocolate, with a hint of opportunity and a dash of—he clicked his fingers, looking for the word—shoe polish?

His eyes snapped open and shot to his shoes, where once again, the shoeshine boy was readying the polish!

"NO," Willy said firmly. "No more shoeshining, thank you very much!" He marched on and the boy scurried off in search of some other shoes.

The arcade was **SPECTACULAR** and lofty, with a lattice ceiling that perfectly framed the winter sky. But Willy soon realized that it was grand in the way grand things tend to be when dreamed up by someone who doesn't do much dreaming. Expensive marble walls, a mosaic floor, gold fittings. As he walked, Willy redecorated it in

his mind. *Caramel walls—no, that's not quite right.*
Scratch-and-sniff walls! Yes! An edible grass floor!
Lollipop door handles! He stopped when he reached
a fusty shop with a queue out of the door. The
chocolates in the window were laid out in unim-
aginative rows, all shaped the same and stamped
with a name Willy knew immediately. It was the
name of one of the most FAMOUS chocolate
makers in the world.

SLUGWORTH

Every box was filled with the same flavor of
chocolate, Willy couldn't help noticing. Plain,
plain, and more plain.

Next to Slugworth's shop stood two equally
fusty shops, owned by the other two famous
names in chocolate making: FICKELGRUBER and
PRODNOSE. But next to them stood an empty shop.

An empty shop with a sign that read: FOR RENT.

Willy stepped toward it slowly, unable to believe his eyes. It was all chipped paint and thick dust. It was a mess of a shop.

It was **PERFECT**.

He could imagine what it would be like to sell alongside the others. The four of them all standing together, a rush of customers, a sea of chocolate-smeared faces and whoops and cheers of sheer delight! Four great chocolatiers and four great friends, side by side. He touched the chocolate bar in his pocket again and suddenly *Wonka* appeared in his mother's writing above the empty shop door! The newspapers plastered over the windows peeled back like curtains to reveal a mountain of chocolates and sweets inside—*his* chocolates and sweets, wild and weird and crowd-pleasingly wonderful.

He took off his hat, pulled a chocolate from it,

and handed it to a passerby. They scarfed the chocolate, and instantly their toes began to tap—slowly
at first, then faster until they were dancing with
gusto! Then another person grabbed a chocolate
and joined in, then another, and another, until
everyone was twirling around. Willy began to
dance too. All around him customers were gulping
down fistfuls of chocolates and **LAUGHING**
and spinning and kicking their legs high in the
air. Willy stood in the middle, marveling at the
magic of it all—they loved his chocolates! It was
his destiny! He had arrived! They really, really
loved—

"*Ahem*," came a cough, and Willy felt a firm tap
on the shoulder. Immediately, the shop melted
back to its empty old run-down state. The people
he had imagined dancing were just shuffling past—
one was even picking their nose.

Willy turned and was **SURPRISED** to see it

was a policeman who had tapped him on the shoulder. He was a young man with bright eyes and the strained face of someone who was trying hard to be tougher than he was. He pointed to a sign in the corner of the arcade.

NO DAYDREAMING

"I'm afraid you'll have to leave," he said, gesturing to the door. "I saw you daydreaming, jumping about, pulling air out of your hat, and trying to hand it to that man picking his nose."

"No daydreaming? *Really?*" Willy said with sincere confusion. "That's very unfortunate because that's what I spend most of my time doing!" He laughed. But the policeman didn't. Instead, he held out a hand.

"And it's a three-sovereign fine."

"Three? Goodness," Willy said, rummaging around in his pocket for the coins. He handed them over. Still confused, he turned to leave and was met with a spray of cologne, right in the face! The shoeshine boy **SMILED** and held out his hand.

"No! I'm not paying you," Willy said. "Not this time."

The policeman raised an eyebrow. "You *will* pay the boy," he ordered as the lad raised his hand higher. "Unless you can find a way to give back that cologne."

"He can't!" the boy said gleefully. "I'll bet it's really soaked into his eyebrows by now."

Willy reluctantly handed over another sovereign, his fingers lingering on the cold coin as the boy pried it from his grasp. Then he made his way slowly to the exit, the usual spring in his step replaced with a disappointed shuffle.

He made for the city's riverbank. A **GOOD** river always made him feel at home. But it was freezing, and the cold was biting at his cheeks.

"The city's colder than I thought it would be, and much more expensive. I can't even make a dozen silver sovereigns last more than one day," he muttered to himself.

Just then, he saw a young mother and her child shivering under a bridge.

"Could you spare a sovereign for a place to sleep?" she asked.

"Oh . . . of course," Willy said, holding out what remained of his coins. "Please, take whatever you need."

She took a silver sovereign from his hand, leaving him with just one left.

He **FLIPPED** his last sovereign into the air and caught it in his coat pocket. Immediately, there was a *clang*, and he looked down to see the coin had fallen through a hole! His final sovereign had bounced off his boot and rolled away down a drain. He frowned. "Well, there goes the hotel."

CHAPTER TWO

SCRUBITT AND BLEACHER

Willy lay shivering on a park bench, too cold to sleep. He'd placed his top hat over his face, but even that wasn't enough to stop his nose from icing over.

He was staring into the dark, empty abyss of the inside of his hat, dreaming up ways to get his shop, when he heard a **KNOCK**. Not just one but three deliberate knocks.

Knock, knock, knock.

He pulled a lever attached to the rim and the top of his hat flapped open to reveal a stocky, broken-toothed man standing over him.

Woof.

And an equally stocky but **EXCELLENTLY** toothed dog.

"You all right there?" the man asked.

"F-f-f-f-ine, thank you," Willy managed. "A little colder than I expected."

"You must be new in town," he said. "I'm Bleacher, and this dog here is Tiddles."

"Willy Wonka. I just arrived. I'm beginning to wish I'd come in the height of summer."

"This *is* the height of summer," Bleacher said, laughing. "You're not planning to sleep there, are you?"

"Unfortunately"—Willy attempted a big frown, but his face was too frozen for it—"I seem to have lost what little money I had. I was planning on sleeping in a nice, **WARM** hotel."

"Ah!" the man said. "Well, as luck would have it, I know someone who can help you."

"Really?" Willy said, his mood immediately warming.

"Yeah!" Bleacher said. "Come with me."

Willy unstuck himself from the frozen bench and shuffled after Bleacher, who was already taking big stalking strides ahead.

"Thank you!" Willy said, hurrying to catch up. "Thank you hugely, sir!"

Bleacher grinned. "Don't mention it. Tiddles and I are always on the lookout for a stranger in need, aren't we, boy?"

Tiddles growled, and Willy clutched his case tighter.

"It's not far," Bleacher said, and he glanced back at Willy.

"Right behind you!" Willy said. "And thawing beautifully with this brisk walk!"

Bleacher grinned. "Good."

"What luck," Willy **MARVELED**. "I'm so glad to have met you."

"Me too," Bleacher said in a voice so close to a growl the dog could've said it. *"Me too."*

Bleacher led Willy through the cobbled alleyways all the way to the outskirts of the city. They walked in silence, and soon the roar and rumble of the city faded into the dark, until all that could be heard was the sound of their echoing footsteps with the occasional growl from the dog.

"Sorry about Tiddles, by the way," Bleacher eventually piped up. "He seems to have taken a liking to your backside."

Willy tapped his chin in thought. "You know! I bet it's not my bottom; it'll be my trousers. They're vintage, actually—I got them from a postman."

"Funny fellow, aren't you?" Bleacher said. "That'll be it. Tiddles would spend all day running after postmen if he could, wouldn't you, boy?"

The dog gave a grunt that sounded surprisingly like a gruff "yes."

Bleacher halted and pointed ahead, down the dark alleyway. "Well, there it is, Mr. Wonka. Home sweet home."

Up ahead was a crumbling building—it was tall, about five stories high, and with every floor Willy's eyes traveled **UP**, the place got more and more lopsided. At the very top, jutting out from the side, was an old wooden bird coop, alive with pigeons cooing hauntingly in the silence. Willy's eyes followed the building **DOWN**, past window frames that had popped out and were hanging there like glassy bats. Some of the windows were barred, and the ground-floor window was shuttered for the night.

"SCRUBITT AND BLEACHER, GUEST-HOUSE AND LAUNDRY," Bleacher boomed as they reached the door.

"Bleacher?" Willy said. "It's you!"

"It's mostly her," Bleacher said, pulling a bell.

Before the bell had even finished dinging, a harsh, grating voice sounded from behind the door.

"If that's you, Bleacher, you'd better have that worm water!"

"Oh, I've got something better than worm water, Mrs. Scrubitt. I've got a *guest*."

There was a *clink* and a *clunk*, and a slot in the door opened to reveal a roving eye.

Willy beamed, and the eye widened hungrily.

"What a charming greeting," Willy said sincerely as the door was thrust open, revealing a squat woman with slicked-back hair. For someone whose job it was to make things clean, she was surprisingly greasy. Her teeth were covered in a gray sludge, and as she **SMILED**, Willy was sure he saw something slimy slither between them.

"Come on in, sir!" she said as Willy tipped his hat to her and stepped inside.

The place was a mess. Bundles of smelly clothes lay on rickety shelves collapsing under the weight of so much washing. The only light—a spiderlike chandelier—was dim and dusty and flickered as Willy moved around the room. He spotted a dumbwaiter in the wall, a **SMALL** elevator-like contraption to carry the washing down to the washhouse. He peeked down the shaft, but he could see nothing but darkness.

"Welcome to Scrubitt and Bleacher, Guesthouse and Laundry. I'm Mrs. Scrubitt, the big boss. You make yourself at home, warm your cockles by the fire. Worm water?"

"Oh, er—" Willy began, but Mrs. Scrubitt interrupted him.

"NOODLE!" she screeched.

Immediately, a sullen and scruffy little serving girl came sliding into the room. She was holding a book in her hand and snapped it shut as she skidded to a halt in front of them. Willy offered her a smile, but she snapped her head away to avoid his gaze— almost as quickly as she had closed her book.

"Put that silly book away and fetch our guest a glass of worm water!" Mrs. Scrubitt boomed. "Poor man's frozen half to death."

Noodle turned her back to them and immediately began busying herself, raising a glass here and uncorking a bottle there. As soon as the cork came out, the most putrid smell filled the room, soaring up Willy's nose and sticking to the back of his throat. It smelled like someone had taken a swamp full of dead things and added mustard and vinegar to it. He began to gag, but much to his surprise, Mrs. Scrubitt was taking great big sniffs

and *ooh*ing and *aah*ing as if it smelled utterly
WONDERFUL.

Noodle pressed a glass of gloopy gray sludge
into Willy's hand and fixed him with an apologetic
stare.

"Worm water," Mrs. Scrubitt said. "There's
nothing more glorious."

"Thank you," Willy said with a **GULP**. He
thought he spotted something slithering through
the gloop. "You and your husband have been . . .
most kind to me."

"HUSBAND?!" Mrs. Scrubitt spat. She turned
to Bleacher. "Oh, you'd like that, wouldn't you?"

"No," Bleacher lied.

"I'm holding out for someone better," Mrs.
Scrubitt explained. "A marquess, or maybe a
prince." She stalked across the room and nudged
the glass of worm water closer to Willy's lips.
"Drink up!"

They both drank and Willy immediately gasped. "That's extremely **POWERFUL** stuff," he managed as something *definitely alive* slid down his throat.

Mrs. Scrubitt licked some stringy gray bits from the corners of her mouth, making a horrible slurping sound between the munching and squelching. When she'd finally gulped down the last drop and licked the glass for good measure, she said, "Now, Mr. Wonka, what can I do for you? A room, is it?"

"Well, yes, but, er . . ." Willy paused, feeling embarrassed.

Mrs. Scrubitt flashed Bleacher a **SMILE**. "You *don't say*, Mr. Wonka."

"I'm afraid it's true, Mrs. Scrubitt," Willy said. "I have not a sovereign to my name. But if my prognostications are correct, all that's about to change."

"Oh yeah?" Mrs. Scrubitt said.

"See, I'm something of a magician, inventor, and chocolate maker. I've spent the past seven years traveling the world perfecting my craft, and first thing tomorrow at the Galeries Gourmet, I plan to unveil my most astonishing creation yet. Prepare to be *AMAZED*, as I present you . . ." He reached into his hat and pulled out . . .

"A teapot?" Mrs. Scrubitt said flatly.

"Huh?" Willy said, before noticing he had indeed pulled a teapot from his hat. "Oh, no, it's not that!"

"They were invented ages ago, mate," Bleacher said.

Willy put the teapot back and started rummaging through his hat again. The others stared as he pulled out a string of handkerchiefs, a bunch of carrots . . . Somewhere inside the hat, an angry *NEIGH* sounded.

"Sorry, it's in here somewhere," Willy muttered. Noodle stifled a **LAUGH**.

"Er . . . don't you worry, Mr. Wonka," Mrs. Scrubitt insisted. "I can see you're a man of great ingenuity, and we've got just the thing for you: the entrepreneurial package! The room's one sovereign a night, but you don't have to pay until six tomorrow. That give you long enough to earn a few pennies?"

"More than enough, Mrs. Scrubitt!" Willy said, *BEAMING*. "Thank you."

Mrs. Scrubitt's lips curled into a sneaky smile. She held out a pen and a contract. "Then just sign here. It's as easy as that."

Willy heard a small cough and turned to see Noodle peering through the hatch to the back room, her eyes wide. She pointed frantically at the contract, grabbed her neck as if she were choking, and then dramatically slumped over as if she had died.

Willy frowned, unable to decipher what she meant. If he . . . *ate* the contract . . . he'd choke . . . to death? Well, he knew that already!

"Read the **SMALL** print!" Noodle hissed.

"Pardon?" Willy said.

Mrs. Scrubitt whipped around and shot Noodle a vicious look. "Thank you, Noodle, that'll be all." And with that, she slammed the hatch shut.

"What was she saying?" Willy asked.

"Who's that, then?" Mrs. Scrubitt said, her voice high and awkward.

"The girl," Willy clarified.

"What girl?" Mrs. Scrubitt said.

"It sounded like *read the small print*, and there's a lot of it . . ." Willy let the scroll-like contract unravel. It unfurled out across the entire length of the room.

"Oh, you don't want to listen to her, Mr. Wonka. She was put down a laundry chute when she was a baby. I took her in out of the **GOOD-NESS** of my heart, and I've done my best," Mrs. Scrubitt explained, "but it's left her with a suspicious nature. She sees conspiracy everywhere."

"Poor girl," Willy said sadly.

"These are all your standard T's and C's, but you're welcome to take a look," Mrs. Scrubitt said, forcing a **GRIN**.

"All right, then," Willy said. "I'll give it a once-over."

Mrs. Scrubitt glanced nervously at Bleacher as Willy read the small print. Carefully, Bleacher pulled a bludgeon from his inside pocket and began creeping up behind Willy.

"Okay, that's . . . Uh-huh . . ." Willy mumbled, running his finger across the contract. "Good . . . Ha! Like what you've done there."

Bleacher slowly raised the bludgeon over Willy's head.

"All right, all right . . . Uh-huh. All right! Well, that all seems to be in order," Willy said.

Bleacher quickly pocketed the bludgeon as, with a **FLOURISH**, Willy signed the contract. He looked to Mrs. Scrubitt, who was as confused as him.

"Oh!" Mrs. Scrubitt finally said, unable to suppress her surprise any longer. "Well, in that case . . . welcome to Scrubitt's, Mr. Wonka!"

Then with an excited skip in her step, she led Willy up a rickety staircase to his room. There were photos of Tiddles and a big poster that read *COME FOR THE NIGHT, STAY FOREVER!* decorating the walls.

"It's utterly charming, Mrs. Scrubitt," Willy said.

"I hope you'll be very comfortable here, Mr.

Wonka," she said with a grin. They had reached the topmost room, and when she opened the door, Willy gasped.

The bed was plump and a four-poster, and there was even a mint on the pillow! A warming fire **CRACKLED** on the hearth, and from up there Willy could see all the domes of the Galeries Gourmet, glinting in the moonlight.

"Sleep well, Mr. Wonka," Mrs. Scrubitt whispered.

As soon as the door closed, she turned sharply on her heel and called sweetly, "Oh, Noodle! Noooodle!"

But while her voice was a charming melody, her face was growing redder and more furious by the second. Her eyes were bulging and bloodshot, and it was clear that she was ready to EXPLODE.

Noodle peeked around the corner. "Yes, Mrs.

Scrubitt?" she chimed, but her face fell the second she caught sight of the raging woman. It was enough to make her little legs shake.

Mrs. Scrubitt charged, grabbing Noodle by the ear with a painful pinch. Then she dragged her screaming along the corridor all the way to the far end and kicked open a heavy door. Beyond it was a freezing, frosty, flapping pigeon coop.

"No!" Noodle squeaked.

"No," Mrs. Scrubitt mimicked with a snort. Her furious hands worked *FAST*, shoving Noodle headfirst toward the riled birds and slamming the door shut.

Noodle frantically scraped at the splintered door, her little fingers slipping through the thick pigeon mess that covered every surface.

She hated it in the coop, and she hated the smell most of all. It was musty and sour and hideously warm all at once, and it never failed to make her retch.

"You ever interfere in my business again, you'll be in that coop all week, understand?" Mrs. Scrubitt growled from beyond the door.

"Yes, Mrs. Scrubitt!" Noodle cried. "Sorry, Mrs. Scrubitt!"

She tucked her knees up under her chin and shivered as the night closed in. There was not another soul in the city with a life more desperate than poor Noodle.

CHAPTER THREE

HOVERCHOCS

The next morning, Willy returned to the Galeries Gourmet.

"LADIES AND GENTLEMEN OF THE GALERIES GOURMET!" he cried. People stopped and stared as Willy thrust his cane against the floor. But when he let go, **AMAZINGLY** the cane didn't fall; instead it stayed perfectly upright—as if it were being held there by magic! People began whispering excitedly and the cluster of customers around him started to multiply.

Delighted yet unsurprised by the awed response, Willy cracked his knuckles and then, with a flourish, pressed a button on the side of the cane. A painful-sounding mechanical whirr emerged from inside, and a flag began unfurling from the top of it—very slowly and with great difficulty.

The crowd inched closer to see more. Willy began wrestling with the flag.

"Imagine the flag bursting from the cane with a BANG!" he told the customers.

People began to leave.

"Aha!" Willy called, getting their attention. "There it is." He pressed the creases out of the flag, revealing that there was a logo **EMBLAZONED** on it—an embroidered *W*. The little letter glinted so brightly, and curved so pleasingly, it drew the crowd in once more.

It was at that moment Noodle happened to be passing, huffing and puffing and dragging a laundry cart at least ten times her size. She stopped to watch. "This should be good," she whispered sarcastically.

Willy cleared his throat. "My name is Willy Wonka," he said, "and I have come to show you a *MARVELOUS* morsel, an incredible edible, an unbeatable eatable—so quieten up and listen down!" He paused. "No. Scratch that, reverse it."

Noodle rolled her eyes.

"I give you," he said, "my HOVERCHOC!" He pulled a jar from his hat and held it aloft, his hand shaking so much the chocolates inside were rattling. They were colored a blinding yellow, with a green casing, split like wings and patterned with red spots. They looked more like magnificent insects than chocolate.

"*That's* chocolate?" someone from the crowd heckled.

"With microscopic hoverfly eggs inside," Willy chimed in response.

"Fly-egg chocolate? Who is this guy?!" someone in the crowd cried.

Everyone was whispering now, and the place was electric with **EXCITEMENT**.

But above the shopping floor, where the owners of the chocolate shops had their offices, it was deadly silent. Three figures had gathered at their office windows to watch the commotion below. Willy hadn't noticed them, but if he had, he would've known instantly who they were. In fact, the whole world knew who they were, because most people ate their chocolate every day: Slug-worth, Fickelgruber, and Prodnose. The three great chocolatiers.

"And when the eggs hatch . . ." Willy went on as he popped off the lid of the jar, "that's when the **FUN** begins."

The smell hit the crowd first and there was a chorus of *mmm*s as everyone inhaled the delicious scent. But then something peculiar happened, something that no one had ever seen happen before. Three little chocolates rose up out of the jar all by themselves and hovered in the air!

Everyone gasped!

Up above, the three famous chocolatiers began to sweat. Slugworth turned immediately to his secretary. "Miss Bon-Bon?" he said. "Call the police."

Back down below, Willy beamed as the customers hung on his every word. It was going better than he had ever imagined; lots of them were licking their lips, and no one could take their eyes off the chocolates hanging in the air. When he thought of his mother, of how proud she would be at that moment, he felt a lump rising in his throat.

"IS IT *CHOCOLATE*?" a small child shouted.

Noodle chuckled.

Willy held out the jar. "Of course it's chocolate. Now, who wants a taste?"

Well, the crowd went wild at that. There were

screams and yelps and people began pulling and pushing, desperate to take a bite. But before Willy could distribute even one of the chocolates, a commanding voice made him stop dead in his tracks.

"I'll have a **HOVERCHOC**."

Willy turned and was delighted to see none other than Arthur Slugworth standing behind him! He knew the famous face very well—he'd seen a photo of him once in a newspaper and had committed it to memory. Slugworth was always there, in his dreams of the future, patting him on the back, welcoming him to the world of chocolate. He was bigger in the flesh, impressive and expensive, clad in a fine suit with **GLINTING** gold threading. He'd once heard that Slugworth always wore a suit, even as pajamas. That was how professional he was.

"Mr. Slugworth, sir!" he said with a bow. "What an honor! Ever since I was a little boy—"

Slugworth grabbed his hand, pumping it up and down in a bone-crushing handshake. Willy winced as two more chocolatier legends fought their way through the crowd.

"**WOW!**" Willy said. "That's quite a hand-shake, Mr. Slugworth!"

"It's a business handshake. Lets people know I mean business. Now, come along." He tapped his watch impatiently. "Tick-tock, tick-tock, get on with all this."

Willy noticed the man's watch had stopped and was going to tell Slugworth that it seemed to be having some trouble with the time, but Fickelgru-ber and Prodnose's arrival distracted him. They loomed over him, not saying a word.

"The chocolate trinity, here in the flesh!" Willy exclaimed, but still they said nothing.

Fickelgruber was tall and spindly—using a handkerchief to wipe his hands.

"I touched a few horrible jackets as I came through the crowd," he eventually muttered to Prodnose by way of explanation.

Prodnose was standing stiffly, as if he had been ordered to do so. He was short and squat and wore a more colorful suit than the others: a mustard tartan two-piece. His toupee was spread flat on his round head with a professional level of slicking. It was rumored the toupee was made from the hair of his late cat, and Willy found himself staring at it. In many ways it was like meeting *four* **FAMOUS** people. He had heard a lot about the cat wig (and most people agreed the cat wore it better).

"Hurry up, boy!" Slugworth boomed. "Let's try one of these so-called Hoverchocs, then."

Willy stepped aside, and Slugworth, Fickelgruber, and Prodnose pushed past, each plucking a floating chocolate out of the air. One after the other, they popped the chocolate into their mouth . . . and one after the other, their faces lit up with exquisite pleasure.

"Ooh! Ooh, it's not just chocolate, is it?" Slugworth said, unable to hide how much he was enjoying it. "There's . . . marshmallow."

"That's right," Willy said, **BEAMING**. "Harvested from the mallow-marshes of Peru."

"And caramel," Fickelgruber added. "But it's . . ."

"Salted," Willy said with a knowing nod. "With the bittersweet tears of a Russian clown."

Prodnose began drooling with delight. "And is that . . . Surely not? Cherry!"

"Cherry *blossom*," Willy corrected him. "Cherry-picked by the pick of the cherry pickers in the Imperial Gardens of Japan."

As they swallowed, the chocolatiers shot each other worried glances.

"Well, Mr. Wonka," Slugworth said, "I have to

hand it to you. I've been in this business a long time, and I can safely say that of all the chocolate I've ever tasted, this is, without a doubt, the absolute one-hundred-percent—"

Willy finally spotted Noodle in the crowd and gave her a thumbs-up.

"WORST!" Slugworth finished.

"Why, thank you, that's very—wait, *what?*" Willy cried.

Slugworth shook his head gravely. "We three are the fiercest of rivals but we agree on one thing. A **GOOD** chocolate should be simple, plain, uncomplicated."

"Whereas this, with all its bells and whistles . . ." Fickelgruber wrinkled his nose. "Well, it's just . . ."

"Weird," Prodnose said.

Willy slumped. He stared out at the captivated crowd, feeling the sting of staring eyes.

"Don't be downhearted, Mr. Wonka," Slugworth

said, stifling a smirk. "So you're not a chocolatier. There are many other lines of business."

"Although I'd avoid fashion!" Fickelgruber snorted.

A **GIGGLE** rippled through the crowd. Willy looked down at his trusty plum-colored coat, and suddenly, he remembered something. His spirits lifted, a mischievous twinkle flashed in his eyes.

"Well, there's one more thing that might change your minds," he said. "But I don't know . . . If you thought the *taste* of my chocolate was weird, you might not like this next bit . . ."

Right on cue, Slugworth's feet left the ground. He was rising up toward the ceiling! His hands were grabbing at air, searching desperately for something to hold on to. But he kept going up and up.

"**WONKA!**" he bellowed.

Willy turned to the crowd and said in his most teacherly of tones, "The hoverfly has broken out of its chocolate cocoon and is flapping its wings like a hummingbird!"

Next Fickelgruber left the ground, and then Prodnose.

"You mean a *fly's* doing this?!" Prodnose screamed.

"Oh, yes," Willy said. "But don't worry; it'll be completely unharmed! In about twenty minutes it'll get tired and exit through your rear."

"Your what?!" Fickelgruber yelled.

"He means we're going to fart them out of our bottoms," Prodnose clarified before flipping over backward and sending his wig falling to the ground.

Willy picked it up, and as he did so, he noticed something curious scrawled inside. Three numbers . . .

"Give me that," Prodnose growled, and Willy hastily threw it back to him. The floating chocolatier caught it and put it back on his head, holding it firmly in place this time so **GRAVITY** couldn't steal it again.

"You're off your rocker, Wonka!" Slugworth shouted. "Who in their right mind would want a chocolate that makes you fly?!"

"Who . . . who . . ." Willy mused. "Let's find out, shall we? Who's for a Hoverchoc?"

At that, the crowd lunged as one—a huge hysterical mass of bodies and outstretched arms, all aimed at the jar. There were screams of delight as Willy pressed chocolates into their hands, and they in turn dropped coins into his pocket. He stood back to behold the marvelous sight as, one by one, they rose upward. More and more of them went up until the great glass dome was plastered with a canopy of delighted customers. A woman in a feathered hat flew past with her dog trot-floating on its leash behind her, followed by a squealing nun doing somersaults. An old man glided along, hands OUTSTRETCHED, laughing so heartily he was raining tears.

Willy stood beneath them, flicking a finger back and forth as if he were conducting an orchestra, his face alight with fun and laughter.

"All right, folks!" came a shout followed by a WHISTLE, and Willy turned to see the police filing in.

"Nothing to see here!" boomed the man at the front. The big boss, the Chief of Police. He was decorated with medals and muscle and had tall leather boots that squeaked as he moved, all arrogant swagger and chest puffed out. He had a fine mustache, which, as he got closer, Willy could see was adorned with little chunks of chocolate. "Just a small group of people defying the laws of gravity," the Chief said. "Hook 'em, boys."

Officers began pulling the floating customers back down to earth, like plucking stray balloons from the sky. Then a familiar face approached Willy—the police officer from the day before.

"I'm not **DAYDREAMING** this time!" Willy said. "No rule-breaking here."

"I'm afraid we've had complaints about you, sir," the police officer said.

"Complaints . . ." Willy paused, waiting for the man's name.

"Officer Affable," he said. "And yes, complaints that you're disrupting the trade of other businesses. I'm regrettably obliged to move you on—and confiscate your earnings."

The Chief nodded to another officer, who marched forward and pulled the coins from Willy's pocket.

"What? Oh no, please!" Willy cried.

"Don't worry, it's going to a **GOOD** cause. Sick kids or something," the Chief shouted over.

"I'm sorry, Mr. Wonka," Officer Affable said. "Rules is rules."

"At least leave me a sovereign," Willy pleaded. "I need it to pay for my room."

Officer Affable glanced over his shoulder to check the Chief wasn't looking, and then slipped Willy a single sovereign from his own pocket.

"Here," he said, then he lowered his voice to a **WHISPER**. "Now, take my advice and sell your chocolate elsewhere."

CHAPTER FOUR

ALWAYS READ THE SMALL PRINT

Willy walked back to the washhouse, his mind whirring as it always did. There was a new chocolate idea or two bouncing about in there, along with a pressing problem to solve. A big one. How to wow at the Galeries Gourmet and convince them to let him sell his chocolates! For as long as he could remember, the **DREAM** of the Galeries Gourmet had kept him going. No matter what sadness or gloom the world threw at him, he could **CONJURE** up that one dream and live in it for a while, and he could wander happily through the last thing he and his mother had imagined together. He wasn't going to let that be replaced with this new memory of heroes who turned out not to be heroes at all. There was always a way to turn things around—he was confident his imagination would conjure up something perfect. It had never let him down yet.

Bleacher was closing the washhouse blinds when he arrived, and Mrs. Scrubitt was inside, sitting in the shadows sipping her stinky worm water.

"Evening, Mr. Wonka," she said. "How'd it go?"

Willy sighed. "Not quite as well as I'd hoped."

"Oh dear," she said, and then she rose eagerly to her feet. "Well, I'm afraid we do have to settle up now."

"Thankfully the room's taken care of," Willy said. "I believe we said a sovereign?"

He pulled the single sovereign from his pocket and placed it on the counter.

Mrs. Scrubitt's eye **TWITCHED** excitedly. "For

the room, yes. But you have incurred one or two extras during the course of your residency with us."

"I have?" Willy said, his nose wrinkling as he desperately searched his mind for what those extras might be.

Mrs. Scrubitt opened her ledger and started totting up his bill.

"Yes, you have. There was that glass of worm water you had when you arrived. And if I remember rightly, you warmed your cockles by the fire."

"He did indeed, Mrs. Scrubitt," Bleacher growled.

Willy looked nervously at the exit as Bleacher bolted the door.

"Cockle warming is extra, see?" Mrs. Scrubitt said.

"Used the stairs to get to his room and all," Bleacher added.

"Oh, well then, you've got your stair charge,"

Mrs. Scrubitt said as she scribbled furiously in her ledger. "And that's per step, I'm afraid, up and down. Now, tell me, Mr. Wonka, did you happen to use the mini bar?"

Willy **RAISED** an eyebrow. "There's a minibar?"

"Mini bar of soap," Bleacher clarified.

"By the sink," Mrs. Scrubitt added helpfully.

Willy winced. "I might have . . . briefly?"

"Ooh-hoo!" Bleacher cried.

"See, even Bleacher knows you never touch the mini bar, and he was raised in a ditch," Mrs. Scrubitt said. "Add in your mattress hire, linen lease, pillow penalty, and you're looking at . . . ten thousand sovereigns."

"I don't . . . don't think you can do that," Willy said, nervously thumbing his cane.

Mrs. Scrubitt flashed him a rotten smile. "All in the small print, deary."

"But I don't have ten thousand sovereigns," Willy said. "I only have one."

Bleacher grabbed Willy by the collar and hissed, "Then we have a problem, Mr. Wonka."

"You'll need to work it off in the wash-house. At a sovereign a day!" Mrs. Scrubitt said **BRIGHTLY**.

"But . . . ten thousand sovereigns," Willy stammered. "That's—"

"Twenty-seven years . . ." Mrs. Scrubitt said.

"Four months . . ." Bleacher grunted.

Mrs. Scrubitt bared her teeth. "And sixteen days!"

Then, before Willy could protest, Bleacher hoisted Willy into the air and *HURLED* him down the laundry chute.

"Aaargh!" he screamed as he slid into the bowels of the washhouse and landed with a *thump* in a basket. He sat squashed among the laundry sacks, cursing himself for not spotting the signs sooner.

"I should've listened to that young girl," Willy groaned. "What was her name?"

"Noodle," came a reply, and much to Willy's surprise, he peeked out of the cart to see an older gentleman in a smart tweed suit standing there. He looked out of place among the mangles and hanging sheets and bubbling vats churning vast lumps of laundry, like someone had plucked him from an office and accidentally dropped him there.

"You must be Mr. Wonka," he said as he pushed up his glasses and then clasped his hands neatly. "I'm Abacus Crunch, Chartered Accountant. At least, I was. Now I, er . . ."

A **TALL** and smiling woman wearing soaked denim overalls came over and thrust out a hand to help him from the laundry basket. "Abacus runs the place," she said as Willy struggled his way out.

"And you'd best do as he says or you'll answer to me. Piper Benz, plumber by trade."

"Accountant, plumber," Willy mumbled, wiping his brow. The air was thick with soap and the whole place was horribly hot.

"And I'm Larry Chucklesworth," came a voice, and a man stepped out from behind a colossal stack of folded towels. He had a curly wig and big bulbous shoes. He spun his bow tie in greeting. "I'm a clown, in case the shoes don't make it obvious enough. Professional clown."

"And this here's Lottie Bell," Piper said, nudging a shy-looking woman forward. Her hair was almost entirely covering her face, like she was trying to hide. "She was a switchboard operator in her day, weren't you?"

The woman said nothing, only **WAVED** shyly in Willy's direction.

"She don't talk much," Piper said.

"So they got you all too, did they?" Willy said glumly.

Abacus bowed his head. "I'm afraid so. Each of us found ourselves in need of a cheap place to stay and neglected to read the small print."

Willy took off around the room, running his hands across the walls, knocking and banging and pulling at pipes. "There must be a way out of here."

"You don't think we've tried?" Piper said. "There's bars on the windows, the dog's on the door . . ."

"And even if you could get out, that contract is watertight," Abacus said.

"Unlike this joke flower!" Larry laughed, **SQUEEZING** some water in his own face. "Sorry, that's a clown joke."

Much to the surprise of the others, Willy spluttered with laughter. "Fantastic!" he said, inspecting the little plastic contraption. "You think it's just a flower, but it's something different entirely! Oh, Larry, I think we will get on very well!"

Larry stared blankly at him, as if a **POSITIVE** reaction was the very last thing he expected.

"I do love ingenious inventions," Willy said. "Especially ones that make a person smile."

"If you're not here at roll call," Piper said, bringing the conversation back to their imprisonment, "Mrs. Scrubitt will call the police, and she'll charge you a thousand for the inconvenience." She sank down onto a pile of laundry and put her head in her hands.

All of a sudden, Tiddles barked from beyond the door, making them all jump with fright.

"All right, everyone, back to work!" Abacus said. "Come on, Mr. Wonka, I'll show you the ropes. You're in this room over here. On suds."

And so everyone returned to their workstations

and Abacus led Willy into the suds room. It was a dingy little room, dominated by two enormous copper vats.

"Your job is to stir, Mr. Wonka," Abacus said.

Willy reluctantly picked up a huge paddle and started **STIRRING** the steaming vat.

"I already think I've had enough of this," he said quietly, but the workers were too busy scrubbing.

***

Time passed slowly down in the washhouse, and though he had only been there for a few hours, it already felt like days. The workers constantly chanting "**SCRUB, SCRUB**" didn't help matters either. Willy found himself repeatedly glancing at the clock, wondering when the nightmare would end. The smell of soap was sickly **SWEET**, and the wet air made him feel itchy.

Finally, after what felt like an eternity, the door was unbolted and Bleacher marched in with a clipboard.

"Bell...Benz...Crunch...Chucklesworth... Wonka," he growled, ticking their names off the list before ordering them upstairs to sleep.

"I'll be sure not to use the mini bar this time," Willy said. "Lesson learned."

"Oh, I wouldn't worry about that, Mr. Wonka. Because you won't be getting any more soap," Bleacher said before grabbing Willy by the scruff of his collar and throwing him into the room. "Lights out in thirty minutes!" he roared as he slammed the door shut.

"A terrifying man, but an Olympic throw on him that I can only respect," Willy said with a shake of the head. He **JUMPED** to his feet and dusted himself off, taking in his new home. The room was very different from the one he had stayed in on the top floor. There was no roaring fire, no treat on the pillow. It was bare, with only a rickety old bed, a small desk, and a small, broken window. Cold air blasted through the cracks in the glass, making an irritating whistling sound, as Willy lay down on the bed to rest his aching bones.

He stared up at the dark ceiling, his stomach grumbling with hunger and his hands stinging from the soap. He was trapped; he . . . felt sure he could hear little footsteps! Impossibly **TINY** ones, like the noise a bird would make if it had purchased some nice loafers. *Tip-tap, tip-tap.*

"It's you again, isn't it?" Willy whispered into the darkness.

But the footsteps **QUICKENED** and disappeared.

CHAPTER FIVE

SILVER LININGS

Willy was finally drifting off to sleep when he heard a loud **KNOCK** at the door.

"Room service!" came Noodle's voice as the door creaked open. She placed a bucket of slops on the floor. "Told you to read the small print, didn't I."

"I know, I know," Willy said. "It's just, well, I'll be honest, I . . . can't."

"Can't what?" Noodle asked.

"Can't read," Willy clarified.

"No! You're kidding me," she gasped.

"Yes, yes," Willy said.

"Your chocolate can make people FLY, and you can't read?" Noodle cried.

"Well," he said, somewhat defensively. "I've been busy with my plan to share Willy chocolates with the world."

"Oh, right," Noodle said.

"For everything else, I've relied on the kindness of strangers."

Noodle laughed a hollow laugh. "And look where *that's* got you—the staff quarters. At least you've got a bed."

Then, as if the bed had heard and wanted to make this day even more grim for Willy Wonka, the whole thing collapsed underneath him.

He hit the ground with a *crunch*.

"I'm okay," he squeaked.

"You *had* a bed," Noodle went on. "A desk and a washbasin—that's also your toilet, by the way. Water comes in two temperatures. Cold and colder."

Willy got up and walked over to the basin—when he turned them on, the dribble of water that came out of each was indeed cold and colder.

"How much do you owe them?" Noodle asked.

"Ten thousand."

"Count yourself lucky!" Noodle said. "I owe thirty."

"What?" Willy said, his eyes WIDENING in disbelief. "How do *you* owe them money? I thought they found you down the laundry chute."

"Oh, they did," Noodle said. "Took me in out of the goodness of their hearts—and charged me for the privilege. You wouldn't have thought a one-year-old could *sign* a contract, but *apparently*, a thumbprint is legally binding!"

"I'm sorry, Noodle," Willy said sadly. "If only you didn't have thumbs—or better yet, if only you'd been put down a nicer laundry chute."

"It's not so bad," Noodle said. "If I keep my

nose **CLEAN**, I'll be out of here by the time I'm eighty-two."

Willy shook his head. "What a pair of monsters."

"That's life," Noodle said. "Cruel and horrible, and folks always choose greed over good deed. It's the way of the world." She tipped some slops into a bowl. "Enjoy your slops."

"Come on, now, Noodle," Willy said. "We're certainly not going to be eating any of *that*."

He went to the other side of the room and fetched his case.

"What are you doing?" Noodle asked.

Without taking his eyes off her, he dropped the case on the desk, making it burst open. It **CONCERTINAED** out like a magic toolbox, expanding and growing pipes on one side and pots on the other! Up popped an array of flasks and beakers—there was a miniature gas stove and a self-stirring wooden spoon.

"Seriously," Noodle said. "What is that? What are you doing?"

"I'm making chocolate, of course!" he said as he began rifling through the strange ingredients. "How do you like it? Dark? White? Nutty? Totally bonkers?"

Noodle shrugged. "I don't know. I've never had any chocolate."

Willy froze.

"What?" Noodle said.

"Never?" Willy said in disbelief. "Not even a nibble?"

"No," Noodle said.

"That's HORRIBLE!" Willy said. "Let's fix that immediately!"

Noodle inched closer. "I'd love to try the one that makes you fly . . ."

"I'm afraid the rest of my hoverfly stock isn't ready yet," Willy said. "Oh! But I do have one or two other ingredients you might like." He cracked his knuckles and began uncorking the jars and tipping things into a pot. "Silver linings will do **NICELY**! Made of condensed thunderclouds and liquid sunlight. Helps you see that faint ray of hope beyond the shadow of despair. Just what we both need, wouldn't you say?"

Noodle watched on, completely **EN-THRALLED**. "Did you always want to make chocolate?"

"I always wanted to eat it," Willy said, shaking some ingredients into the pot on the stove. "Back when I was your age, my mama was the cook. We didn't have much money, but each week, she bought one cocoa bean, and by the time my birthday came around, there was enough to make an entire bar of chocolate. And it wasn't just any old chocolate; it was the best. She knew a *secret* no other chocolatier knew, not even Slugworth. It was a secret that made her chocolate the best in the world!"

Noodle leaned in closer, her eyes wide. "What was the secret?" she asked.

"I never got a chance to ask her," Willy said sadly.

"What . . . happened to her?" Noodle whispered. Willy's eyes were **GLISTENING** with tears.

"She died," he said in a whisper. "Very suddenly. There was no one to look after me, so I boarded a ship, and after years traveling the world, here I am."

Noodle put a hand on his shoulder. "What was she like?"

"Magical," he said. "She's the reason I'm here—in a way."

"Well, yeah," Noodle said. "That's how it works."

Willy gestured around him. "No, *here*, making chocolate."

"What do you mean?"

"We dreamed up coming here and selling chocolate together. I've held on to that dream because,
well, my mum once promised that when I shared
chocolate with the world, she'd be right there
beside me. And I know it sounds silly, but I've
always hoped somehow she'll keep that promise.
She might even tell me her secret!"

The case PINGED and Willy leaped from foot
to foot excitedly.

"They're ready," he said, reaching into the pot.
Noodle watched eagerly as he pulled out a perfectly
formed chocolate. He shook it in the air to cool it a
little. "Here," he said, throwing it over to Noodle.
"Try!"

Noodle caught it and cradled it gently in her
hands. It was a white chocolate, shaped like a cloud
with a **BEAUTIFUL** glistening bolt of lightning
running through it. She lifted it to her lips and
nibbled a small bite. Then stopped.

Willy leaned closer, gazing **HOPEFULLY** at her.

"Well?" he said.

"I wish you hadn't done that," she whispered.

"Why not?" Willy asked urgently. "Don't you like it? I really thought you would like it!"

"No, I like it," Noodle said. "It's just . . ."

Willy leaned closer. "What?"

"Now each day I don't have chocolate will be a little harder," she said.

"Oh!" Willy said, and he breathed a sigh of relief. "*That*, Noodle, is exactly how you should feel after eating chocolate." He paused, an idea forming. "How would you like to have all the chocolate you can eat every day for the rest of your life?"

"A lifetime supply?" Noodle said, sounding skeptical.

"A lifetime supply," Willy confirmed.

Noodle raised a suspicious eyebrow. "What would I have to do?"

"Not much," Willy said. "Just get me out of here."

Noodle **LAUGHED**. "Don't be ridiculous!"

"Shh! It's easy!" Willy said, and then he began excitedly pacing the room. "I'll get someone to cover my shift and you can smuggle me out in your laundry cart—just for a few hours, mind. Nobody would even know I was gone!"

"What's the point of that?" Noodle said.

"To sell chocolate, of course!" Willy said. "We'll split the profits and pay off Mrs. Scrubitt in no time!"

"It's a nice idea, Willy . . ."

"It's a great idea!" he corrected her.

Noodle's face grew serious. "But it'll never work."

"Of course it will," Willy said dismissively. "Now, eat the rest of your chocolate."

She popped the rest in her mouth. "You don't

understand," she said as soon as she'd **GULPED** it down. "Mrs. Scrubitt's like a hawk. She keeps her beady eye on everything that comes in and out of the washhouse. Except . . . huh."

"What is it?" Willy asked eagerly.

"No, it's nothing," Noodle said, shaking her head in surprise.

Willy shrugged. "Oh, okay."

". . . Huh!" Noodle said.

"Ah! That's the double-huh!" Willy cheered. "That's not nothing. That's the silver lining at work. It's given you an idea!"

"Okay," Noodle said, her eyes suddenly wide with **EXCITEMENT**. "So the one time she's ever dropped her guard was when this aristocrat came into the laundry. Had a castle he couldn't find his way back to or something and ended up here. He was only asking for directions, but she was all over him like a rash. It was disgusting."

"That's it, Noodle!" Willy cried. "All we have to do is find her an aristocrat and slip out while she's distracted."

He popped a silver lining in his mouth.

"Yeah, but where are we going to find an aristocrat?" Noodle said.

"Huh," Willy said instantly.

Noodle moved closer. "Huh?"

"Huh!" Willy said again.

"A double-huh!" Noodle cried with delight.

"Have you got a pencil and paper?" Willy asked quickly, his eyes darting around the room in search of one. "Because I've got a **MARVELOUS** idea . . ."

CHAPTER SIX

THE VAULT

In the dead of night, the Chief of Police walked alone through the town square. His big leather boots crunched loudly against the frosty ground and his pace was slow but deliberate, like he had walked the route a million times before. He passed the frozen fountain and made his way to the cathedral, his mustache **TWITCHING**, eyes wide as if he were possessed. When he reached the door, he raised his fist and pounded the wood in a strange series of knocks.

The door creaked open and out flooded the sound of Latin chanting. Monks, barely visible in the flickering candlelight, glided up and down the aisles as if they were flying.

"Keep up the chanting, fellas," the Chief said. "You sound **TERRIFIC**."

He quickened his pace, eyes fixed on a confession booth in the far corner. It was an ornate box, divided down the middle and housing two seats, which were concealed by a heavy curtain. The Chief was so large he had to squeeze himself into the booth sideways. He plonked himself down and, turning to the priest waiting inside, said, "Forgive me, Father, for I have sinned" in a humdrum tone, as if he wasn't even really trying. "I have had a hundred and fifty of these chocolates since my last confession." Then he did a peculiar thing—he slid the priest a chocolate.

"Temptation is very hard to resist," the priest whispered as he took the chocolate and inspected it, giving it a sniff.

"You can say that again," the Chief said.

The priest gave the chocolate one final sniff and nodded his approval. Then he pulled a lever on the wall. Immediately, the whole confession booth rumbled and grumbled like an old car, and the Chief's side of the booth began to lower. The Chief crossed his legs and sat back casually, as if it were the most normal thing in the world. **S L O W L Y** , like an elevator, it descended and disappeared under the floor.

The Chief emerged into a crypt lit by dim candlelight and was greeted by a guard.

"Evening, Chief," she said as she unbolted a thick metal door and pushed it open for him.

Beyond was a corridor lined with pipes, valves, and gauges, like the bowels of a factory. The Chief strolled through **CONFIDENTLY**. He knew where he was going. Soon, the corridor opened up into a room where, cocooned in three tall armchairs, sat three familiar figures.

Slugworth finished scribbling in a smart green ledger and looked up at the Chief. Next to him, Fickelgruber was making himself a chocolate martini, and Prodnose was aggressively biting into an ice cream. Standing behind them was Miss Bon-Bon, Slugworth's secretary. She was busily flicking through some paperwork and raised her eyes only momentarily to acknowledge the Chief's presence.

"Good evening, all! I bring my invoice," the Chief said, brandishing a piece of paper. "One chocolatier moved on for the usual fee."

Miss Bon-Bon took the invoice. Slugworth handed her the green ledger, and she placed the invoice inside it very carefully. Prodnose threw the Chief a box of chocolates.

The Chief's eyes were suddenly alight with chocoholic **DESIRE** and grew so wide and hungry, they looked like they might escape from his head and get to the chocolate first! His mouth became a swampy mess of saliva as he lunged for the box.

"Ooh, yeah, that's the good stuff," he purred as he scooped the chocolates into his greedy fist. "Is there a second layer? Yeah, there is! And a third? . . . No, that's just box."

"How would you like to earn a few more of these?" Slugworth asked.

The Chief nodded, his mouth now too chock-full of chocolate to speak.

"We think Mr. Wonka requires more than just 'moving on.' He's good," Slugworth muttered.

"**TOO GOOD!**" Prodnose added.

"What's more, he only charges one sovereign a chocolate!" Fickelgruber cried. "So *anyone* can afford them! Even the . . . the . . ."

"The poor?" the Chief suggested as he gulped down the last of the chocolate.

Fickelgruber retched and raised a handkerchief to his mouth.

"He doesn't like it when people say 'poor,'" Prodnose explained.

Fickelgruber retched again.

"Sorry, Felix," Prodnose said, patting his accomplice's shoulder. "Sorry for saying 'poor' *again*. And again just now."

"Stop saying it!" Fickelgruber pleaded.

"We want you to send Wonka a 'MESSAGE,'" Slugworth said, ignoring the others.

"Backed up by physical force!" Prodnose shouted.

"That if he tries to sell chocolate in this town again," Slugworth said, "he's liable to meet with a little 'accident.'"

"In which he dies," Prodnose clarified.

Fickelgruber waved his handkerchief. "You don't have to *say* it. We all know it's a death threat."

"Just making sure we're all on the same page," Prodnose said.

"No one's on your page, Prodnose," Fickelgruber muttered under his breath.

Prodnose began to rise out of his chair. "What's that supposed to mean? Well, I *know* what it means—actually, what *does* it mean? What even is a page? None of us are on pages . . . Are we talking book pages?"

"Gentlemen, please," Slugworth said. "Let's keep it to business, shall we? So, what do you say? Do we have a deal, Chief?"

The Chief stood still. The empty box in his hand started to shake. "Now, look here, fellas. I've always been **HAPPY** to help in the past . . ."

"And you've been handsomely compensated . . ." Fickelgruber said.

"And I appreciate that, really . . . really I do," the Chief said, stumbling a little over his words. "I love your chocolate, especially those little orange ones with the dots on? They sure go down smooth—but that's not the point! The point is, I'm an officer of the law. And lately I've been wondering if all this criminality is really suitable for someone in my position."

Slugworth's eyes NARROWED. "I see."

"I can't just go 'round roughing up your competition," the Chief said quietly. "I'm sorry."

The chocolatiers exchanged looks, and slowly they rose from their tall chairs, like snakes in long grass.

"Well now, Chief, I'm glad to see you're a man of integrity," Slugworth said. "But how about . . ." He leaned closer. "A hundred of your favorite chocolates?"

The Chief strained to resist, gritting his teeth. "I'm actually trying to cut down on chocolate, you know, to get in shape for the police officers' ball."

Slugworth offered his hand. "*Seven hundred* boxes?"

The Chief's eyes briefly lit up. "That's a lot . . ." he said, his fingers twitching in eagerness to do the deal. "I'm sorry, NO!"

Slugworth flipped a big switch on the wall. Suddenly it was **RAINING** chocolates! Great big ones were thudding down all around them. Slugworth offered his hand again and whispered enticingly, "*Eighteen hundred boxes?* It's more than most could eat . . ."

The Chief stared down at Slugworth's hand, and he found that, finally, he could resist the chocolate no more. Morals were one thing, but this was *chocolate*. So much chocolate.

"DEAL!" he cried.

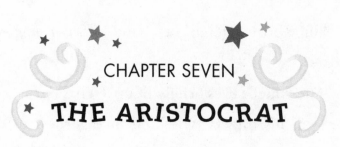

The gentle sound of dawn birds **SINGING** was shattered by an earsplitting whistle.

Willy stepped out of his room, rubbing his eyes, as one by one the workers from the washhouse lined up for roll call beside him. He had walked into the room the night before feeling broken—but Noodle had made him remember that people *needed* his chocolate, and he shouldn't let anyone, Scrubitt or Slugworth or whoever, steal his dreams. And so he spent the entire night wide awake, running through all the possibilities of escape. The people of the world needed him to make chocolate, not scrub their laundry. If only no one had to do the laundry . . . If only there was someone, or *something*, who would gladly give it a whirl . . .

"Bad first-night's sleesp, huh?" Piper said, wincing at Willy's exhausted face.

"Oh yes, not a wink," he whispered. "I drew a made-up aristocrat, and then I couldn't stop DREAMING about the possibilities of today!"

Piper turned to Abacus. "He's cracked already."

"Bell! Benz! Crunch! Chucklesworth! Wonka!" Bleacher shouted, and the workers dutifully filed down the stairs to the washhouse.

"Bleacher!" Mrs. Scrubitt cried out as they passed. "Toilet's blocked again!"

Bleacher rolled his eyes.

"Ah!" Willy said, taking his chance. "The unmistakable sound of love."

"The what?" Bleacher snapped.

"Don't tell me you haven't noticed?" Willy

whispered. "She's madly in **LOVE** with you!"

Bleacher stared at him for a second, then said with a snort, "Mrs. Scrubitt?!"

Willy put on his most serious face. "Besotted," he lied. "And why not? Look at you: a fine figure of a man. You just need to tidy yourself up a bit, get some new clothes, have a bath."

"What's a bath?" Bleacher said.

"Oh . . . a bit of a scrub. A splash around in some soap. Like the laundry!" Willy explained. "You could also consider a nice new outfit—show off the legs."

Bleacher stared off into the distance, and Willy knew then that whatever little cogs Bleacher had up there in his skull, they were now most certainly turning. "Mrs. Scrubitt would be **WOWED**," he added, just to make sure.

"Get in there!" Bleacher cried, shaking his head as if he were shaking the nonsense out of it. He shoved Willy down the stairs to the washhouse.

But as he sauntered off with an unmistakable spring in his step, Willy felt certain the plan was afoot . . .

★★★

Upstairs, Mrs. Scrubitt marched into the shop and screamed. "Bleacher?! Did you **HEAR** what I said about the toilet being blocked? Curse that idle peasant! It's a worm-water fiasco in there!"

She stopped when she saw Noodle standing in the middle of the room. She wasn't folding laundry—instead she was intently studying a piece of paper.

"What's that?" Mrs. Scrubitt sneered.

Noodle immediately whipped the paper behind her back. "Nothing, Mrs. Scrubitt."

Mrs. Scrubitt put her hands on her hips and

sneered. "Do you like the coop, Noodle?"

"All right!" Noodle cried in mock surrender, holding out the piece of paper so Mrs. Scrubitt could see it. "I was collecting laundry from Professor Monocle the other day. He's writing a book about the Bavarian royal family. Got sketches of noblemen all over his wall. And this one looked . . . rather familiar."

Mrs. Scrubitt took the bait. She tore the paper from Noodle's hand and inspected it.

For a moment she was silent, and Noodle worried she'd figured out the truth—that it was a drawing she and Willy had cobbled together, nothing more. But then suddenly the woman burst to life. "HOLY WORM WATER," she *GASPED*. "IT'S JUST LIKE . . ."

"Mr. Bleacher," Noodle said, nodding furiously.

"Are you telling me *Bleacher's* a Bavarian aristocrat?" Mrs. Scrubitt screeched.

"You can't deny there's a certain quiet nobility to him," Noodle said, trying not to laugh.

Mrs. Scrubitt stared off into the distance, a dozy smile spreading across her face. A smile was spreading across Noodle's face too. Then suddenly, Mrs. Scrubitt snapped back to reality. "What have you got to smile about?" she spat at Noodle. "GO GET MY WORM WATER!" She aimed a kick at Noodle, which sent her scurrying away.

Immediately, Noodle peeked back around the door, worried Mrs. Scrubitt had come to her senses. But instead, the horrible woman was **HUGGING** Willy's scrappy drawing and sighing!

Only a few hours later, the smell of fancy soap wafted through the corridors of the washhouse, followed by heavy footsteps.

"Oh, FINALLY!" Mrs. Scrubitt shouted. "Bleacher, the toilet, I have been calling for you all morning, where have you be—" She stopped talking and her jaw **DROPPED**.

"Where'd you get them dungarees?" Mrs. Scrubitt asked, looking from Bleacher to the drawing and back again. He was wearing shorts so tight his thighs squeaked as he moved, and he'd combed his hair into a neat little quiff.

"Found it all in lost property. Why?" he said smoothly. "Suit me?"

"Not bad," Mrs. Scrubitt rasped, trying to keep her cool.

Bleacher shifted awkwardly, trying to smile sweetly but in fact just baring his teeth. "Mrs. Scrubitt," he said. "Can I just say, your eyes are like two . . . rabbit droppings in a bowl of custard."

"Oh, my lord!" she oozed. "You'll make me blush!"

"Fancy some worm water, you . . . maggot?"

Bleacher said, uncorking the bottle with his teeth.

Mrs. Scrubitt grabbed the bottle and took a swig, then let the stringy water dribble down her chin as she grinned up at him.

He plucked a particularly juicy worm bit from her chin and lifted it slowly to his mouth, ripping it with his teeth, making Mrs. Scrubitt shiver with **DELIGHT**.

Noodle stood by the door with her fist in her mouth, trying not to laugh—and also trying not to be very, *very* sick.

★★★

Unlike upstairs, down in the washhouse everything seemed to be as it was every day—nothing but scrubbing.

Then Willy appeared, skipping out of his section.

He began to load old bits of laundry equipment into a laundry cart—ropes, a mangle, rollers.

The workers watched him as he **HEAVED** the cart across the room and disappeared with it back into his section. As soon as the door closed, loud bangs and clangs sounded.

"I told you he'd lost it," Piper said, shooting Abacus a worried look.

The workers inched closer until their ears were pressed against the door.

"Should we go in?" Larry whispered as the bangs grew louder. "I could tell a joke and cheer him up?"

Suddenly, the door flew open and Willy strolled out. Much to their surprise, his trousers had a perfectly cut square hole in the bottom.

Nobody said a thing, they just watched as Willy opened the door and held up the missing piece of fabric.

"Oh dear," Piper said. "He's a dead man."

Tiddles the dog shot through the air, a mass of muscle and teeth and furious drool. Willy ran round and round in circles as Tiddles gave chase, and the others watched on helplessly.

"**WOO-HOO!**" Willy roared. He ran one more lap and then pelted into his section with Tiddles in hot pursuit.

The door slammed shut, and from beyond it came growls and barks and tearing sounds and the clang of metal.

"Oh, what's that sound?" Abacus fretted.

"We've got to do something!" Larry said. "But all I can offer is jokes."

It was Lottie who, without saying a word, stepped forward and kicked open the door. They all ducked, bracing for a dog attack, but nothing came.

When they finally looked up, Piper burst into hysterical **LAUGHTER**.

Willy had assembled a mass of ropes and pulleys and pipes to create a huge, hulking machine, all powered by Tiddles running in what looked like a big hamster wheel. Just beyond the dog's furious jaws, the square from Willy's trousers dangled enticingly on a string.

"Ladies and gentlemen, may I present a brand-new contraption of my own creation. An innovation in laundrification!"

The workers' jaws were on the floor.

"Let me ask you a question," Willy said. "How does Tiddles want to spend his time? Running after posties! Now, with Willy Wonka's Wild and Wonderful Woof-o-Matic Wonka-Walker—don't make me say it again—he gets to run while I have fun."

"It's genius," Piper said with an approving nod. "You're a genius, Wonka."

"Right, now that's done, I'm just popping out for a bit," Willy said, then he sauntered over to the dumbwaiter that carried the freshly washed laundry back up to the shop.

"You can't just leave," Piper said. "This ain't no hotel."

"I'll be back by roll call," Willy said, then he jumped in the dumbwaiter, grabbed a laundry bag, and **WRIGGLED** into it, pulling it up to his neck. "While I'm away, Tiddles has kindly agreed to scrub!"

The dumbwaiter rolled up and out of the washhouse, and his gobsmacked friends waved a feeble goodbye.

With a *ping*, Willy arrived in the shop to find Scrubitt and Bleacher **GIGGLING** together in the corner. Mrs. Scrubitt was sitting on Bleacher's knee asking things like, "How many jewels do you own?" and "What's 'castle' in Bavarian?"

He was replying with answers like, "Is this stone in my shoe a jewel?" and "What's Bavarian?" but she was too enamored to notice.

Noodle raced up, her face a picture of pure delight. She shoved Willy's head down into the bag and heaved him into the cart.

"Right under Scrubitt's and Bleacher's noses!" she whispered as the pair of them rolled on out of there into the afternoon sun.

Once outside, Willy quickly climbed out of the cart and dusted himself off.

"I can't believe it worked!" she said.

"Now, for the next part of the plan," Willy said. "Wait till you see how much chocolate I made last night!" He began rummaging in his hat. "We sell this, and then—oh no!"

He held an empty jar aloft and eyed it suspiciously.

"What's going on, Willy?" Noodle said. "Where's the chocolate?"

"Not again," Willy said, with a dramatic roll of the eyes. "I don't know how to tell you this, Noodle, but . . . the chocolates have been stolen."

"Stolen," Noodle said flatly, a sledgehammer of suspicion in her voice.

"**MMM-HMM**," Willy said.

Noodle crossed her arms. "Who by?"

"The little orange man," Willy said gravely.

"What?" Noodle exclaimed.

"The little orange man with the green hair. Didn't I tell you about him?" Willy said. "He's my nemesis, Noodle! He's about yea high, comes in the dead of night, quiet **LITTLE** footsteps, *tip-tap, tip-tap*, and then he steals all my chocolate. Been happening every few weeks for the past, oh . . . three, four years now."

Noodle narrowed her eyes. "Really."

"Oh, yes," Willy said. "Sometimes I spy him in that strange realm twixt sleep and wake, green hair glinting in the moonlight. One day I shall capture him, Noodle . . ."

"Willy?" Noodle said slowly.

"And when I do . . ." Willy went on.

"Willy?!" Noodle cried. "You don't actually expect me to believe you, do you?"

"Of course I do!" Willy said. "What other explanation could there be?" He **WAGGLED** the empty jar in her face.

"I don't know," she said. "That you go to sleep, dream about a little green man—"

"Green hair," Willy corrected her.

"And while you're dreaming . . . YOU STUFF YOUR FACE WITH CHOCOLATE!"

Willy gasped! "How dare—Actually, that does make a lot more sense. Have I been eating my own chocolate?"

Noodle threw her arms in the air. "Why did I ever think this would work?"

Willy was still lost in thought. "I don't *think* so. I'd know if I ate my own chocolate in my sleep, surely . . ."

"Stupid silver linings," Noodle said.

"Hey!" Willy said. "There's nothing stupid about my chocolate."

"If Mrs. Scrubitt had spotted us, I'd be in the coop right now!" Noodle cried. "Do you have *any* idea what that's like?"

"Look, Noodle, I'm sorry, okay? But it's just a setback. We can make more chocolate. The only problem is, I'm all out of milk . . ."

Noodle swiped a bottle of milk from the nearest doorstep. But Willy quickly took it off her and put it back.

"Firstly, that's stealing, Noodle," he said sternly. "And thirdly, Willy Wonka does not use any old cow's milk. For this particular creation, I require the milk of a giraffe."

"Why a giraffe?" Noodle asked.

Willy flashed her a **SMILE**. "So my chocolates are head and shoulders above the competition."

Noodle opened her mouth to comment but realized it was easier not to.

"Fine," she said. "As a matter of fact, there's one at the zoo."

"**FANTASTIC!**" Willy said, strutting off down the alleyway.

"But firstly," Noodle said, "the zoo isn't that way."

"Gotcha," Willy said, changing direction.

"And secondly," Noodle said, "they're not just going to let you walk in and milk it!"

Willy stopped dead in his tracks and held his cane aloft. He tapped the small golden globe on the top of it and immediately it sprung open, revealing a tiny, perfectly wrapped chocolate box.

"That, my dear Noodle," he said with a mischievous smile, "is why we're very lucky the little green-haired man didn't find this."

CHAPTER EIGHT

THE PARTY CHOC

In a ramshackle hut beside the zoo entrance, a security guard eyed Willy's little chocolate box with suspicion.

"What is it?" he said.

"A gift from Zoo Management," Noodle said with **ENTHUSIASM**. "In recognition of your years of service!"

The security guard lifted it, going cross-eyed as he tried to focus on the tiny packaged chocolate.

"I've only been here a year."

Noodle shifted awkwardly. "Which . . . is why there's only one small chocolate."

"Oh, that makes sense," he said.

"It does," Noodle said proudly.

"Well . . . thank you very much," he said, and with that, he closed the door.

Noodle darted back to the nearby bush, where Willy was crouched, waiting.

"Good work," Willy WHISPERED. "Now we wait."

"What does it do?" Noodle asked, craning her neck to see through the hut's window. "Is it a flying one?"

"No, no flying this time." Willy beamed. "I can't wait for you to see it." They sat in silence for a moment, then Willy added, "Of course, it is just a prototype, and I've never tried it before, so I can't guarantee that even I know what is about to happen."

Noodle put her head in her hands.

"It's called the Party Choc," Willy said, rubbing his hands together in anticipation.

Noodle shot him a look. "What does it do?"

Suddenly, there was a bang from inside the hut and the security guard leaped to his feet.

"It recreates the perfect party—food and drink and a *DASH* of entertainment."

The security guard immediately started running in impossibly fast circles.

"Ah, it's possible that I haven't quite got the measurements right yet . . ." Willy mumbled. "He's started running about with his friends—Oh, look, now he's munching through an entire plat-ter of party food. He'll be tasting all the flavors, filling up on cream puffs and little gummy sweets and licorice and—"

"Smoke!" Noodle cried.

Indeed, steam was coming from the man's feet now and filling the security lodge. Willy inched forward, readying to intervene, but all of a sudden the man slumped into his chair and began making a slurping sound.

"Now he's having a nice **FIZZY** drink, and then it's on to the birthday cake."

"Look, I think he's getting sleepy," Noodle said excitedly.

"I'm sure I added another layer . . ." Willy mused just as the security guard leaped to his feet and started bouncing—impossibly high, right to the ceiling, and back down again.

"Ah, the **BOUNCY** castle," Willy said. "No party is complete without one."

Noodle looked impatiently at her watch.

Then came the crying, big sobs and wails.

"He's feeling the big feelings now, because he doesn't want to leave the party," Willy said, doing a sad lip.

Noodle shot him an exasperated look.

"And finally," he said, rising expectantly to his feet.

There was a muffled thud.

"Bedtime."

Noodle's eyes grew **WIDE**. "You mean . . ."

"Partied out," Willy said with a satisfied nod.

★★★

Willy and Noodle made their way through the zoo, shining torches to illuminate the path. They passed a lake filled with flamingos.

"Why don't they fly away?" Noodle mused.

"I don't know," Willy said. "Perhaps they haven't thought of it."

A sign for giraffes pointed them in the direction of the TALLEST building in the place, and once inside they slipped down a corridor lined with feeding buckets and straw and special doors for the zookeepers to access the enclosures. Willy inspected each door sign carefully, looking for the one marked "giraffe."

"Where are we? Giraffe . . . giraffe . . . giraffe . . . Ah!" he exclaimed, wrenching a door open with confidence.

"WILLY!" Noodle screamed. "That door is marked '*TIGER*'!"

Willy couldn't see a thing in the darkness beyond the door, but he could suddenly feel hot breath . . . the brush of a whisker . . .

Noodle slammed the door closed. "You have *got* to learn how to read!"

"Why?" Willy asked.

"You were nearly eaten by a tiger!"

Willy raised a finger pointedly in the air. " 'Nearly' is the key word there, Noodle. I've *nearly* been eaten by a lot of things. And none of them got more than a nibble."

"Giraffe," she said, tapping a sign on the next door, and then opening it.

Inside, a giraffe LOOMED large, all spindly legs and knobbly knees. Its long neck catapulted its head toward them like a crane swinging cargo into dock. It fixed its eyes on Noodle.

Noodle gulped.

Its eyelashes were batting fast, as if it didn't believe what it was seeing.

Willy doffed his hat in greeting. "Good evening—a little late for visitors, I know, Mrs. . . ."

Noodle read the sign. "Abigail," she said shakily. "She's called Abigail."

Well, the giraffe didn't like that. It threw its head back and reared up, flashing the underside of its hooves. Its nostrils flared and snorted a warning. Noodle bolted backward in panic, slipping and sliding and landing with a squelch on the muddy floor before she could reach the door. As she desperately tried to struggle to her feet, Willy **WAVED** his hands at the giraffe and said urgently, "Whoa there! Easy, now." He turned to Noodle. "And you too. The giraffe won't hurt you." Then he reached into his pocket and pulled out a small knobbly green sweet.

"What's that?" Noodle asked.

Willy held it closer to the giraffe. The animal started sniffing, and instantly it dropped back onto four hooves and became all FRIENDLY, nudging Willy and nibbling at his hat.

"It's an acacia mint," Willy explained as the giraffe pinched one from his palm and chewed on it. He slowly reached a hand up and began scratching its ear. "There we are, there we are," he said soothingly.

Noodle inched closer, her eyes wide with wonder.

"Giraffes are just crazy about my acacia mints, see," Willy said, gesturing for Noodle to join him.

"Love them more than anything else. Except being scratched behind the ears, of course."

The giraffe raised its head and gave Noodle's face a huge lick.

"It's tickly!" she squealed with **DELIGHT**.

"Now, Miss Abigail," Willy said, "we have a favor to ask of you. If my colleague here scratches your ears, could you possibly spare us a pint or two of milk?"

Only seconds later, Willy was sitting on a stool, milking the giraffe, while high up above him Noodle **WOBBLED** at the top of a rickety ladder, scratching the animal's ears, just as promised.

"Have you done this before?" Noodle asked, beaming at the magic of it all.

"Oh yes," Willy said. "Without the giraffe milk, my giraffe-milk macaroons would be much shorter."

Noodle snorted and shook her head. "You sure can be silly, Willy."

"I suppose that's true-dle, Noodle."

"True-dle?" Noodle laughed.

"That doesn't work, does it?" Willy mused. "But nothing rhymes with Noodle. Where'd you get that name, anyway?"

Noodle tensed. "Doesn't matter."

"It does," Willy said. "Go on."

But Noodle didn't say a word.

"You don't have to tell me if you don't want to," Willy said. "If it's a secret."

There was silence for a moment, but when Willy looked up again, he saw Noodle had stopped scratching the giraffe's ear and was instead *CRADLING* her necklace with both hands.

"It's all I have from my parents," she said quietly. She climbed down and handed the necklace carefully to Willy.

He turned it over in his hand, inspecting it closely. An amber and gold ring hung from the chain, and something was engraved on it.

"It's an *N*," she said quietly. "*N* for Noodle. Or Nora or Nina—or nothing at all."

"Can't you trace the owner?" Willy asked.

"You don't think I've tried?" Noodle said. "I've been to every jewelry shop in the city. For years I hoped I would find them, but now I know I never will."

Willy pushed the milking stool to the side and stood up. "Don't say that, Noodle."

"You know, I used to dream that when I found them, they'd live in this beautiful old house, full of books for me to read. And my mom would be waiting for me at the door. I'd run into her arms and I'd finally feel like I was home. And the **HUG** would feel like it could last forever, but it *actually* would, because once I knew what that hug felt like I could hold on to it . . . forever."

A lump formed in Willy's throat as he remembered his own mother's big, tight hugs. He could still feel her **WARMTH** and the chocolate smell of her apron, how she'd rest her chin on his head and SQUEEZE so tightly.

"But then I realized it was just a stupid dream," Noodle said, and she shook her head as if she were shaking all the dreams out of herself. "Right, that's the whole sad story. Now let's get back to milking."

"You must never let anyone or anything steal a dream like that away from you," Willy said seriously. "There's nothing stupid about it."

"Isn't there?" Noodle said. "My parents put me down a laundry chute and never came back. Fact is, they didn't want me. That's all there is to it."

"I know things haven't been easy for you, Noodle," Willy said gently. But they're going to get better. I'm not going to let you rot in that washhouse forever."

Noodle looked up at Willy, her eyes searching for a reason to believe him. "You promise?" she choked.

"I can do better than that," Willy said, standing tall. "I pinkie promise." He held out his hand and they hooked pinkies. "And that's the most solemn vow there is," he whispered.

Noodle quickly wiped a tear away and beamed at him.

"Now get scratching," he said as Noodle began to climb back up the ladder. "We don't have long until the guard comes to-dle, Noodle—to-dle?"

"That still doesn't work," Noodle said, giggling.

Willy **SMILED**. "Doesn't, does it? I'm working on it. Ah, and we are finished! Now, care to dance to celebrate?"

Noodle shook her head, so Willy started

dancing, leaping from foot to foot and waving his arms.

He spun the ladder and Noodle clung on for dear life! But then, taken with the moment, and **SWEPT** up in the magic of Willy's infectious enthusiasm, she launched herself into the air and landed on the muddy ground with a *squelch*.

Together, Willy and Noodle danced out of the enclosure, spinning through the zoo, past pandas and polar bears and penguins and puffins; they shimmied through the snake section and twirled past the tigers. Willy grabbed a huge bouquet of balloons from a stall and the sheer size of it was enough to lift them up high into the air!

Their dancing feet skimmed over the still water of the lake and the flamingos craned their necks to watch. Then, as if the idea had just come to them, the birds flapped their wings and rose up, engulfing Willy and Noodle in a flurry of pink feathers.

He could just make out Noodle's amazed expression between the constant slaps of wings to the face.

Snow began to fall all around them, but though it was freezing, Willy felt so **GLORIOUSLY** warm.

Across town they all flew, Noodle and Willy and an entire zoo supply of flamingos, dancing over the cathedral's rooftop and all the way past the domes of the Galeries Gourmet, before touching down by the fountain in the town square.

The air was still, aside from the huge flock of flamingos (who were really flapping up there), and the town was fast asleep. Willy and Noodle looked at each other, their faces full of mischief, and then they tore off around the square, galloping around the fountain, **SINGING** and **DANCING** and shrieking with laughter.

But not everyone was sleeping. A certain

Officer Affable was making his rounds at the far side of the square. He caught sight of Willy over by the fountain and raced to the nearby pay phone.

"Chief? You know that fella you wanted a word with? I think I've found him."

Noodle skipped around and around in circles, laughing, while Willy cheered.

Suddenly, a whistle sounded and they both froze. Willy looked up to see the Chief marching into the square, accompanied by Officer Affable.

"Mr. Wonka!" the Chief bellowed, making even Affable jump. "A word in private, if I may."

"You'd **BEST** get out of here," Willy said to Noodle, nudging her away.

"But—" Noodle began.

"Don't worry, Noodle," he said. "I've talked my way out of tighter spots than this. I'll meet you back at the cart. We can't have the milk confiscated, now, can we?"

Noodle looked down at the bottles of milk in her hand and knew Willy was right about that. She gave him a dutiful nod before charging off down the street.

Willy stood shivering, hands in his pockets, as he waited for the officers to crunch their way around the fountain. The wind was picking up and it was bitingly cold. It felt like blades on his cheeks.

"You be on your way, Affable," the Chief said gruffly as they reached Willy.

Officer Affable paused. "Are you sure, sir?"

"This is between me and Mr. Wonka."

Officer Affable hesitated.

"Affable!" the Chief bellowed. "LEAVE US."

With that, the officer turned on his heel and *SWIFTLY* headed back the way he had just come. Willy eyed the Chief expectantly, but the man didn't say anything. Instead, he waited, watching, until Officer Affable had got in his car and driven out of sight. But even once he was gone, the Chief didn't move—he just stood there, fidgeting, sighing, as if gearing himself up for something.

"Now, if this is about Abigail . . ." Willy started as soon as they were alone. But before he could finish, the Chief grabbed him by the collar, dragged him through the snow, and shoved his face into the fountain. Willy's nose broke through the ice, and his ears filled with freezing, gurgling water. He gasped and heaved with the fright of it, but though he wriggled with all his might, the Chief's iron grip held him under.

"I've got a message for you, pal," came the Chief's warbled voice. "Don't sell chocolate in this town!" And then he pulled Willy back out. "Got it?!" he said with a **HOPEFUL** stare.

Willy spluttered. "Not really, I'm afraid."

"Oh, you got a mouth, huh? I said . . ." The Chief grabbed him again and pushed him back under. "DON'T. SELL. CHOCOLATE!"

He wrenched him out again and this time Willy's legs seized up from the cold and gave way. He landed in a heap and said, "No, I don't have a mouth on me! Well, I *do* have a mouth." He was desperately trying to catch his breath. "But I was underwater, so I couldn't hear what you said!"

"Oh. Yeah," the Chief said, helping Willy to his feet. "I'm sorry, I'm all outta whack." He lowered his voice to a whisper. "The chocolate is making me do it! Truth is, I don't really want to be here."

Willy CLUTCHED his head—it felt so painfully numb he could barely think. "Neither do I," he said. "I don't think I want to be here anymore either."

The Chief's face brightened. "There you go, then. We got that in common. But I gotta give you a message: sell chocolate again in this town, and you're gonna get more than a bonk on the head."

"I haven't had a bonk on the head," Willy pointed out.

"Oh!" the Chief said. "What is wrong with me? Would you mind please removing your hat?"

CHAPTER NINE

THE GREEN LEDGER

B ack at Scrubitt and Bleacher, Noodle pushed the cart containing Willy back into the washhouse, right under Mrs. Scrubitt's nose.

"Ow, my head," Willy groaned as she made her way to the laundry chute.

"Keep it down back there," Noodle hissed. But it didn't matter; Mrs. Scrubitt was too busy **STARING** into Bleacher's eyes.

"And your eyes," she was saying, "are like tomatoes that someone's sat on."

Bleacher grinned awkwardly. "I don't get to see my eyes much because they're busy doing the lookin'. But I'll take your word for it."

"Oh, you're so **POETIC!**" Mrs. Scrubitt sighed. "My poetic lord."

Noodle heaved Willy into the laundry chute and he slid back down to the washhouse—it was like he'd never left.

"Mr. Wonka!" Abacus cried as he arrived back with a thud. "Good of you to join us."

"Not late, am I?" Willy asked.

Abacus inspected his watch. "No. Cutting it a bit fine."

"Why are you soaking wet?" Piper asked suspiciously.

"Went for a dip in the fountain," Willy said as he made his way to his section. "Tiddles been pulling his weight?"

"As a matter of fact, Tiddles is a **MARVEL**," Abacus said. "Productivity is up thirty percent!"

"We took the afternoon off," Larry chimed in.

"But that's not the point," Abacus said.

"This is the point!" Larry said, pointing and nodding at his own finger.

"Not now with the 'jokes,' Larry," Abacus said wearily.

"Sorry," Larry mumbled.

"The point is," Abacus said, "where have you been, Mr. Wonka?"

"What've you been up to?" Larry added.

Piper sniffed the air.

"And why do you smell of giraffe?"

Lottie leaned in, eager to hear Willy's answer.

"Guess I do owe you an explanation," he said as Noodle wandered in with a mop and bucket. "Truth is, I have not given you the full story. I'm actually a chocolate maker chasing a dream and Noodle has been helping me."

"He's not just any chocolate maker," Noodle said. "He's the best in the world!"

"Oh, Noodle, you're flattering me." Willy blushed. "But she's right. My creations are **PERFECT**."

"The plan is to sell chocolate and pay off Mrs. Scrubitt. At least, that was the plan, until . . ." Noodle trailed off.

"Let me guess," Abacus said. "You had a little run-in with the Chief of Police."

"How did you know?" Willy cried in surprise.

"Because that's what happens to anyone who tries to sell chocolate in this town," Piper said.

"Why?" Noodle asked.

"Three reasons, Noodle," Abacus said, holding up his hand and counting them on his fingers as he listed them off. "Slugworth. Fickelgruber. And Prodnose."

"I thought they were rivals," Noodle said.

"Ah!" Abacus said. "That's what you're meant to think. The truth is they're working together, as a sort of chocolate cartel, if you will."

Willy slumped on a pile of laundry and put his head in his hands. The situation was worse than he thought. "How do you know all this?" he asked.

Abacus sat down next to him, a guilty look washing over his face. "Because I was Slugworth's accountant. For one week . . ."

They all leaned in **CLOSER**, eager to hear the tale.

"One morning, I got a call—some **FANCY** chocolatier's bookkeeper was off sick, so I was asked to fill in," Abacus said, speaking slowly so the others wouldn't miss a single detail. "It seemed like a straightforward job. Until I realized there were two sets of books for his accounts—one for the authorities, and one that told the truth. I discovered the real one when, one night, I brought the ledger I'd been working on to his office and found the place was empty—everyone had already left for the night. I was going to leave too, but then I saw another ledger on his desk, only this one was green and the one I had been working on was red. Of course, I took a look at the other ledger, it was my job—if there were more accounts to go through, I didn't want to miss them. And, *well*—"

"Yes . . . ?" Willy said, leaning in closer.

Abacus lowered his voice to a whisper. "That's when I realized the man is a crook! Slugworth, Prodnose, and Fickelgruber have been watering down their chocolate and storing it in a secret vault deep beneath the cathedral, guarded round the clock by a corrupt cleric and five hundred chocoholic monks."

Willy and Noodle *GASPED!*

"I dare say no one else knows this, but their operation is wilder than anyone could imagine," Abacus said. "There were dodgy invoices, receipts and blueprints showing how they funnel chocolate from their three factories into the secret vault. They use it for bribes, blackmail, and bludgeoning the competition! The entire city is under their control."

"Can't we do something about the chocolate?" Noodle said, looking to Willy for an answer. "If they didn't have the chocolate, well . . ."

"The chocolate is guarded like **PRE-CIOUS** treasure," Abacus said. "Even if you got past the priest and the monks, the vault in which it is kept is accessed by a secret elevator, secured by a nine-digit code that changes every day. And the code is never kept in one place—it's split between the three of them. They each possess only three of the digits so none of them can get at the chocolate without the others."

Willy and Noodle exchanged worried glances.

"I stayed until dawn reading the ledger," Abacus

continued. "That's when I heard footsteps—it was Slugworth! I dived under the desk just in time. He took the ledger and said, 'Miss Bon-Bon, I'm taking this to the vault.'"

"Of course he was," Willy said, shaking his head. "To hide it, no doubt."

"And that's not all," Abacus said with a **GULP**. "When Slugworth reached the door, he stopped. Then he said, with more malice than I have ever heard a person season their words with, 'Mr. Crunch? You're fired.'"

"Oh dear. He knew you were there, that you had seen it!" Willy exclaimed.

Abacus nodded gravely. "So then of course I went straight to the police, and I told the Chief everything. But they'd already got to him. I was arrested and charged with Slandering a Captain of Industry and Hiding Under a Desk—I was fined every penny I had."

"I don't believe it!" Willy said, staring off dreamily into the distance. "I always thought hiding under a desk would get you a lengthy jail sentence."

Everyone turned to look at him.

Noodle, who was used to Willy's eccentricities by now just smiled fondly and said, "Continue, Abacus."

"All I needed was somewhere to lay my head until I could work out how to get back home," he said sadly. "I lay on a bench by the canal, and that's where Bleacher found me. That was four years ago."

The others all moved to comfort him, **HUDDLING** close, making sympathetic noises.

"I'm sorry, Mr. Wonka," Abacus said. "But judging by that lump on your head, the Cartel regard you as serious competition—and they've got you right where they want you. You can't afford a shop without selling chocolate, and in this town, you can't sell CHOCOLATE without a shop."

CHAPTER TEN

A MAGIC TRICK

That night, Willy sat in his room in a cloud of chocolate, hammering and molding and throwing ingredients over his shoulder into a gloopy mixture.

He was more determined than ever to share his chocolate with the world. He couldn't let some crooks stop him, and more importantly, he couldn't let poor Noodle down.

The mixture was soon ready, and he walked to the window, squeezed his head through the bars, and whispered, "Psst—Noodle!"

Immediately a light flicked on in the window next door, to the left of Willy's.

"What is it, Willy?" she said sleepily.

He swung a line of rope across to her. "Watch out! Catch!"

Noodle's hand shot out and caught it with ease.

"Good catch!" Willy whispered. Then he grabbed a basket and threaded the handle through the rope and sent it across. "Now look inside," he said, craning his neck to watch Noodle. She pulled a jar of chocolates from the basket. They were so *FRESH* and still so warm that they'd steamed up the jar. She tilted it up and down, trying to see what was inside.

"Your wages," Willy said. "A lifetime supply of chocolate, remember?"

Noodle **SMILED**. "You didn't have to do that."

"Nonsense! I gave you my word."

"Well . . . thanks," she said. "I've got something for you too." Then she rolled up a piece of paper and put it in the basket, sliding it back to him.

"For me?" Willy said, the gesture catching him off guard. The basket hit his window and he fished out the little ripped piece of paper. There was something scrawled on it—sort of pointy, with a couple of legs like the milking stool. He held it upside down and much to his relief he figured out what it was. "It's a drawing of a glass half full. Thank you, Noodle. I do feel this perfectly captures our attitude these past few days; we could very easily have given up, then you delivered me some slops and reminded me that I am Willy Wonka and I—"

"It's an *A*," Noodle said, interrupting him. "You know? The first letter of the alphabet? I'm teaching you to read."

"Oh, Noodle . . ." Willy said, holding the piece of paper to his heart and hugging it. "You have already given me so much. Honestly, I think I'm going to find reading impossible, but it's a **NICE** gesture."

"You *will* learn," Noodle said firmly. "I can't have my business partner being eaten by a tiger . . . or *nearly* eaten."

"So we're business partners?" Willy asked excitedly.

Noodle shrugged casually. "Well, sure, but I don't know how we're going to sell any chocolate. Every time the police show up, you'd need to disappear into thin air."

"Like a magician," Willy gasped, and soon a great big grin was spreading across his face. "But magicians use lots of *stuff*—cards and rabbits and ropes and pulleys and trapdoors . . . and we don't have any of those."

The light in the room next to Noodle's flicked on.

"As a matter of fact, you do," Piper said.

"What?" Willy and Noodle said at once, leaning out as far as they could so they could see her.

"There are trapdoors all over the city," Piper explained. "They're called storm drains. I'd be **HAPPY** to show you around—if you cut me in on the action."

Willy felt a flurry of excitement. "Are you sure, Piper? You'd be at great risk."

Piper rolled her eyes. "Listen. One day, I was at Slugworth's installing a coffee machine, and this old drifter came by and asked me for a cup. I gave him one. And Slugworth saw me. Had me fired. I ended up here. So yeah, you better believe I wanna stick it to the Cartel."

"Okay, then," Willy said with a grin. "Welcome to the team." And then he threw Piper a chocolate.

"Mm-hmm! That is some good chocolate!" Piper said. "For that, maybe I'll even show you the storm drain I don't show nobody."

The light flicked on in the room next to Piper's. "Hey," came Larry's voice. "If you're recruiting, you can count me in. I don't have any practical skills, but I can talk like I'm underwater. **BLOOGURGLY** bubble-glug, I'm under-water, blup-blup."

Willy clapped. "I was transported, Larry, really, I was. You're in!"

"And if you need someone to handle communications, I'm your woman," came a voice in the darkness.

They all froze, and there was a long pause.

"Lottie?" Noodle finally said.

"I did not know she could speak!" Piper cried as they all leaned out of their windows to see if it really was Lottie.

"Why are you all staring at me?" Lottie said.

"I thought you were a mime," Larry said. "A very, very good mime."

"No, just **QUIET**," Lottie said with a shrug. "Back when I worked at the telephone exchange, I was quite the chatterbox. Since I came here, I haven't had much to shout about."

"That's all going to change!" Willy cheered.

The light in the room next to Lottie's flicked on. "I'm sorry to pour cold water on all this fun," came Abacus's voice. "But if Mrs. Scrubitt catches you trying to escape, she'll add five thousand sovereigns to each of your bills, so just think about that before getting involved in this hare-brained scheme."

"But it's *not* harebrained, Abacus!" Noodle protested.

"And, may I remind you, there is a lot of work to be done in the washhouse," he went on.

"I actually had an idea that could free up your time to join us," Willy said.

"Oh, come on, Abacus," Noodle said, and she lobbed a chocolate in his direction. "Willy's chocolates are **INCREDIBLE**. Try one."

Abacus caught it and popped it in his mouth. "That's very kind of you, Noodle, but I don't care how good his chocolates are, I—" He froze, and his eyes **WIDENED** with wonder. "When do we start?"

CHAPTER ELEVEN

YOU'VE NEVER HAD A CHOCOLATE LIKE THIS

The very next day, they put their plan into action. As soon as the sun rose in the *WATERY* sky and the city square came alive with activity, Noodle was there in the middle of it all with her cart. The others climbed out of their laundry sacks and assumed their positions.

Piper ran down an alleyway, Larry stood on watch at one end of the square and Lottie at the other. Abacus was in charge of the payment jar, and Noodle kept watch by Willy. He was barely recognizable in a disguise of black trousers and a white shirt. He held a serving tray as if he were a waiter, and, one by one, he built a little pile of chocolates on top of it. No one was paying him the slightest bit of attention, and Willy couldn't help but hop about in the snow—the freedom of being in disguise and the suspense of what was about to come was making him want to break into **DANCE!** Next to them, cart owners were organizing their wares for the day, stacking vegetables and perfume bottles and all sorts of other things.

The flower-stall owner, however, was having a very different morning than the rest of them. Willy immediately noticed what was going on and sidled closer as a man on one knee raised a ring up to her, his cold, doughy hands wobbling—thoroughly unprepared for this moment.

"Oh, I don't know, Colin," the stall owner said. "You're a lovely man and all, but I'm looking for someone to sweep me off my feet, you know?

Whisk me off to a life of **ADVENTURE!** Could that be you?"

"Mmm . . . no, Barbara," Colin said.

Barbara's face fell. "Oh," she said. "That's a shame."

"Not with my chronic lack of self-confidence, I'm afraid!" Colin said, then he got up and dusted the snow off his knees. "I'd best be off."

"B-but Colin . . ." Barbara stuttered.

"I'm sorry to have wasted your time, Barbara. Taxi!" He stuck out an arm to hail one, but the driver carried on as if he didn't notice him at all. The car's tires skidded through a puddle, splattering Colin in a thick coating of snow and mud.

Willy moved closer and plucked a perfect macaroon from his tray. It was patterned like a giraffe and topped with little ears.

Colin sniffed it with great suspicion.

He took a cautious bite of the macaroon, and

instantly he stood **TALLER** with a newfound confidence. Then he began to dance!

In seconds, a crowd was upon them.

"*Chocolate for all!*" Willy cheered as they waved their money at him.

Suddenly, a whistle sounded. Willy turned to where Noodle was keeping watch by the fountain. She whistled again and pointed frantically down a side street. Willy's heart sank as he saw the Chief and his officers rounding the corner and charging toward them.

Quick as a **FLASH**, Willy turned and ran down an alleyway.

"*I've never had chocolate like this!*" came Colin's cries of joy behind him.

Willy picked up his speed, racing fast to where Piper was waiting up ahead. She was sweating and her muscles were aching as she held up the heavy manhole cover.

"Your trapdoor, Mr. Magician!" she joked, as Willy slid past her and dropped down into the storm drains. He looked up to see Piper inching the cover back into place. The sound of scraping metal was soon replaced with silence as the last sliver of daylight disappeared and he was submerged into darkness. Within seconds he could hear the thundering footsteps of the police above. They ground to a halt.

"You seen a man, about yea high, probably acting oddly and singing about chocolate?" came the muffled sound of the Chief's voice.

"No, sounds like someone I'd remember seeing," Willy heard Piper reply, and it made him chuckle. He skipped off through the tunnels, the **CHEERFUL** splash of his steps echoing around him.

★★★

It was like a whole other world down there, deep under the ground. As the days passed, the underground passageways became like a home to him. He would skip about with jars of chocolate, tipping his hat to rats as he passed by. In fact, Willy was able to get all over town using the storm-drain tunnels, and soon he was popping up everywhere. His mysterious appearances were all anyone was talking about—everyone wanted him to magically materialize next to them. The whole city was *desperate* for Willy chocolates.

But Willy was becoming increasingly hard to spot, thanks to his many disguises. One day, he boarded a tram dressed as a ticket inspector with a boxy beige hat and matching jacket. He'd prepared a new recipe, all singing and dancing in its ingredients, and wanted to try it out. The fast-moving tram seemed like a sensible place, because if anything went wrong, the people would be contained inside (hopefully). It was PERFECT!

"Look! Look! I've got a Wonka chocolate!" a lady on the tram cried with joy as Willy placed a **LUMINOUS** red chocolate in her palm. All the other passengers were up out of their seats immediately, shouting and squealing, "IT'S HIM!" They stretched their arms out, pleading for him to hand them a chocolate too.

"Just one bite and you'll be dancing to your own tune!" Willy said, and the passengers watched in amazement as the woman who had just scoffed the chocolate began to dance. She threw her arms in the air and started kicking her legs. Willy threw the contents of a jar up into the air and everyone jumped, catching the falling chocolates—some straight in their mouths! Soon the whole tram was singing and dancing—some sedately, others were flinging themselves around with wild abandon.

One woman in particular was doing repeated high kicks and knocking everyone's hats off. Willy sat down at the back of the carriage crossing his legs and reclining with a satisfied sigh. He stared down the aisle at the commotion of his own making and felt **DELIGHTED** with himself.

The washhouse workers were always nearby— Lottie and Larry kept watch, Piper was on storm-drain duty, identifying the best escape routes, and Abacus managed the money. Noodle's job was to help Willy hand out the chocolates.

Of course, every selling day always ended abruptly, with one of the washhouse workers sounding the alarm and the Chief charging in.

When the tram ground to a halt at its stop, the Chief climbed aboard. But Lottie was quick: she sounded the alarm with two sharp whistles and Willy immediately raced over to Piper, who raised a hatch in the floor. From there, Willy dropped down and straight into an open storm drain below.

"He was just here!" the Chief roared in fury as he began throwing passengers left and right in frustration. "Where did he go?"

The passengers carried on singing and dancing as the Chief's face turned POSITIVELY purple with fury.

★★★

It's fair to say the Chief was more than a little baffled as to where Willy was disappearing to and exhausted with the constant hunt. On top of it all, he was having to deal with an increasingly irate cartel, who were watching their chocolate sales plummet.

On another day, Willy emerged from a manhole and strutted into a barbershop, his hands held aloft. In each fist was a **DELICIOUSLY** creamy éclair topped with what looked suspiciously like a real mustache.

"Try my éclair, sir!"

"What's it made of?" a balding customer asked.

"Well, chocolate," Willy said. "And a single drop of yeti sweat."

"A single drop of yeti sweat?!" the customer cried.

"It doesn't sound like a lot," Willy said. "But anything more than a *single drop* would have some dire consequences."

"But . . . A YETI?!" the customer screeched.

In the local school playground, Willy sold spiraled *springy* sweets, which launched the children skyward to impossible heights and then *boinged* them back down to the ground again, with all limbs intact!

Willy watched as they disappeared into the clouds, the squeals of delight raining down on him, and he smiled.

All across town people were singing Willy's praises and talking about his extraordinary chocolates.

And all the while, Willy skipped through the drains beneath their feet—though it was dark and dingy and dripping with sewage, he had never felt closer to his dream.

★★★

While during the day the washhouse workers **STEALTHILY** sold chocolate, by night Noodle and Willy focused on reading. Every evening she stood over him as he squatted on a child's school chair, his face contorted with confusion—Willy was *not* the easiest student to teach.

Soon, though, the group had so much money, the prospect of escaping the washhouse was looking more and more likely.

But one day, while handing out chocolates in the town square, Larry raised the alarm.

The Chief was charging across the square, colliding with carts and throwing people out of his way. The workers scattered and Willy dived down an alleyway and into a storm drain.

"They were just here!" the Chief wailed. He stood there, spinning in the square, his face squished in confusion. All around him people **DANCED** with chocolate-smeared mouths. The Chief was just about ready to explode when something caught his eye—something glinting by the drain. He got down on all fours so his face was practically touching it. A chocolate! But not just any old chocolate; it was a Wonka chocolate. And better still, half of it was squashed *under* the manhole cover.

"Oh, so *that's* how you're doing it," he said, and a thin smile S T R E T C H E D across his face.

He lowered his head and pressed an ear to the ground. The sound of footsteps made him smile even more. "Affable, I want an officer at every storm drain in the city."

"Are you sure, sir? Shouldn't we focus on all those unsolved murders?"

"No, this is the priority," the Chief said. "You skip off for now, Mr. Wonka," he said. "You skip off for now . . ."

CHAPTER TWELVE

GOTCHA!

As the city slept that night, a minuscule figure scurried up to the laundry. Stealthily, they pulled a contraption from their pocket—a little metal bow with a large hook on a wire. They **RAISED** it in the air, pulled a trigger and, quick as a flash, the hook shot through the night and hit the bars of Willy's bedroom window with a little *ping*. The figure pulled at the wire to check it was secure and then began to climb.

When they got to the top, the figure slipped through the bars with ease and dropped down onto the floor. *Tip-tap, tip-tap*, they crept past

Willy, who was **HUMMING** a happy tune between snores as he dreamed of chocolate rivers and chocolate trees.

The tiny figure scurried to the far side of the room and came to a stop next to a jar of chocolates on the floor. They stepped out from the shadows, revealing a flash of green hair, raised their arms greedily, took another careful step forward, and—

SNAP!

The floorboard shot up, hitting the figure in the face and sending them hurtling across the room! They hit the wall, then dropped down into a masterfully placed funnel, which in turn fed into a glass jar. As soon as it landed, the jar lid snapped shut, trapping the figure inside.

"GOTCHA!" Willy roared as he leaped out of bed and hurried over to inspect his catch.

"Let me out of here!" the figure shrieked.

Willy practically fell over. "You can talk!"

"Of course I can talk, you fool. Now let me out of here! I demand to be released!" He kicked the glass angrily.

"Not till I take a good look at you," Willy said, lifting the jar onto his desk and flicking the light on. "The little orange man with the green hair," he said with SATISFACTION. "I *knew* I wasn't eating my own chocolate in my sleep. So you're the funny little man who's been following me."

The figure puffed out his chest indignantly. "Funny little man! How dare you! I'm a perfectly respectable size for an Oompa-Loompa."

"An Oompa what, now?" Willy said.

"In fact, in Loompaland I'm regarded as something of a **WHOPPER**," he boasted. "They call me Lofty. So I'll thank you not to keep gawping at me like something you found in your handkerchief. I find it uncomfortable and, frankly, rude."

"I'm very sorry," Willy said.

"And let me out of here!" the Oompa-Loompa shouted. "You've no right to go around bottling up innocent strangers."

"Innocent?" Willy cried. "You've been stealing from me for years!"

The Oompa-Loompa wagged a finger at him. "You started it! You stole our cacao beans!"

"What are you talking about?" Willy said, his face growing worried. "I would never steal."

"You mean you don't even remember?!" the Oompa-Loompa cried. "That's even worse!"

"Remember what?!" Willy said.

The Oompa-Loompa pressed his face against the glass until his nose was completely flattened, and then, very gravely, he said, "The night you ruined my life."

"I do not remember that *at all*," Willy said. "Are

you sure it happened? Perhaps you've mis-taken me for someone else."

"My job in Loompaland is guarding our cacao beans," the **OOMPA-LOOMPA** said with a huff. "We don't have many; it's not a great place to grow cacao. Then one night you came along and stole them all!"

Willy frowned, thinking hard. He flicked through all his adventures in his mind. But there were so many, and he couldn't think of any that were like—He gasped! He recalled the little boat, the perfect island bathed in sunlight. He remembered picking the big cacao beans!

"Why didn't you say anything?" Willy said. "I would've stopped if I'd known."

"Well, perhaps I drifted off!" the Oompa-Loompa said, grimacing. "I woke up and my **FRIENDS** were standing over me, and they were furious. They sent me away. Disgraced. Cast out in the cold. Until I pay them back, I can never return home."

"Look, Mr. Loompa," Willy said. "If you really think years of thieving my chocolate is a reasonable penalty for taking three beans—"

"Four!" the Oompa-Loompa corrected him.

"—then I'm sure we can come to an understanding, but I can't just hand over my entire supply," he explained. "I've got other people counting on me."

"All right," the Oompa-Loompa said, his eyes shifting suspiciously. "I'll tell you what. You let me out of here, and we can discuss it like grown-ups."

"Oh, that would be **MARVELOUS**," Willy said. "Let's do that."

"Just . . . take the lid off the jar," the Oompa-Loompa said slowly.

"Of course," Willy said.

His eyes narrowed as Willy flipped the lid off and let him climb out.

"Thank you," the Oompa-Loompa said, dusting himself off. "Now, would you be so kind as to pass me that miniature frying pan?"

"This one?" Willy said, reaching over to a set of little frying pans hanging from his case.

The Oompa-Loompa's eyes narrowed further. "The heavy one."

"All right," Willy said, handing him the pan.

"Ooh, that's quite a beast, isn't it?" he said, turning it over in his hand. "Now, come a little closer. Closer. Come on, **COZY** up now."

Willy moved closer, and closer, until—

THWACK!

"Aaargh!" Willy screamed as a horrible ache spread across his forehead. "You hit me!" he cried. "An accident, I'm sure, Mr. Loo—"

But the Oompa-Loompa was too busy stomping. He stomped up and down on each of Willy's fingers, making the chocolatier squeal. Then he grabbed the jar of chocolates and hopped up onto the window ledge.

"OOMPA-LOOMPAS DO *NOT* NEGOTIATE!" he roared. "Good day, sir!"

And with that, the Oompa-Loompa disappeared into the night.

CHAPTER THIRTEEN
THE SHOP

The next morning, Noodle dragged her cart out of Scrubitt and Bleacher and headed for town. To anyone who passed her, it must've looked like she was speaking to the laundry.

"He came back?" she said, sounding unconvinced.

The laundry bag Willy was hiding in **WIGGLED**. "Yes, Noodle!"

"A little green man?" came Abacus's confused voice from his laundry bag.

"Green hair," Piper corrected him from her laundry bag. "Orange man."

"Yes!" Willy said. "I set a trap and he walked right into it!"

Noodle stopped the cart. "So where is he, then?"

There was a **LONG** pause and then Willy said, "Oh well, we had a fight, see? He won. Hit me with a frying pan, then stomped on my fingers before taking the chocolates and jumping out of the window!"

"Of course," Noodle said flatly, then she tapped the cart to let them know the coast was clear.

"You don't believe me, do you?" Willy said as he climbed out.

"Honestly?" Noodle said. "No, not one bit."

"Do *any* of you believe me?" Willy asked.

The others all stared at him with a look of intense **FASCINATION**, like small children watching a monkey misbehaving at the zoo.

"No," Abacus admitted.

"Nope," Piper said.

Lottie shook her head. "Um, no."

"Noooo," Larry said.

Noodle smiled a mischievous smile. "But as it so happens, we don't need to sell chocolate today."

"We don't? Why?" Willy asked.

"You know that shop?" Noodle said. "The one you've been dreaming of?"

Willy's heart stood still.

"Well . . ." Noodle said, and she held up a set of keys.

★★★

They went immediately to see the place, hurrying through the Galeries Gourmet. When they got there, Willy stared down at the keys glinting in his hands. He could hardly breathe.

"These are more than keys to a shop," he said,

in shock at what his friends had done for him. "They're the keys to my dream."

"Legally speaking, it's just a shop, but yes, emotionally, it is also your dream," Abacus said with a matter-of-fact tone.

"Oh, let him have this moment," Piper said, and Willy was sure he even spotted a tear in her eye.

"I can't believe such **KINDNESS** exists," Willy said, his voice cracking as he said it.

"The chocolatier who can make people fly can't believe in this kind of kindness?" Noodle laughed. "Surely not."

Willy **SMILED** at each and every one of them. "I haven't felt this feeling since I was a young boy at home," he said, and he placed the key carefully in the lock and turned it. The door creaked open and together they all stepped inside.

Willy stood with his hands on his hips, surveying

the place. It needed sprucing up, that was for sure. The wallpaper was peeling off the walls, and most of the ceiling was on the floor, along with a smashed chandelier.

"It does need work," Abacus said.

"Looks like someone left the water on twenty years ago and the ceiling fell through," Piper mused. "And the ceiling above that, and the ceiling above that . . ."

"But that means we can afford it—for a week, anyway," Abacus clarified.

Willy felt Noodle's anxious eyes on him.

"What do you think?" she whispered. "Will it work?"

"It's a horrible mess," Willy said. "I've never seen a shop in such a dreadful state. It's absolutely, horrendously . . . *perfect*. I mean, sure, it's a wreck, but look at the potential—the bones. This is going to be the *BEST* chocolate shop in the world. We won't need more than a week, Abacus. We get this right and we'll sell so much chocolate, we'll be free by Friday!"

The very thought made Noodle's eyes well with tears, and she flung her arms around Willy and squeezed him tightly.

"All right," Abacus said. "But we're not out of the woods yet. We'd best get back to the washhouse before roll call."

CHAPTER FOURTEEN

THAT GIRL

The workers emerged from the storm drain by the washhouse. But this time, they were not alone. In a neighboring window stood three sinister figures, and next to them stood a chocolate-snaffling Chief of Police.

"There's six of them in total," he said, his mouth **BULGING** with chocolate. "Including the little girl. She seems to be the brains of the operation. The others do what she says, look."

They all watched in silence as Noodle ordered the workers into laundry sacks and then heaved the cart through the door.

"And that there is the laundry. Scrubitt and Bleacher, it's called," the Chief said, shoving another fistful of chocolate into his mouth.

Slugworth looked up sharply at the name. "Scrubitt's?" he said.

"Mes, Mubitt's," the Chief managed between big chews. He **GULPED** the mouthful of chocolate down. "Why? You know it?"

Slugworth stared dead ahead. "Yes," he said. "As a matter of fact, I do."

The Chief shook the empty box of chocolates and mild panic flashed across his eyes. "Oh no, gone already." He fidgeted, fighting the urge, but it was no good. "You know," he blurted out, "I'm happy to do whatever you want to get rid of them all—and I mean *anything*. They just rented a shop, so legally I can't touch them, but *illegally* I'm happy to do whatever you guys want. You want them *all* to have a little accident?"

"In which they die," Prodnose added.

"No problem," the Chief said. "But it's gonna cost you a lot more **CHOCOLATE**."

"All right, Chief . . ." Slugworth said, waving a dismissive hand. "You can have more."

"And I'd be grateful if I could have an advance, 'cause those other boxes you gave me? They're all gone," he said. "Everything's gone."

"What?" Fickelgruber cried. "All of them, Chief?"

"Yep. I've run out! I've been eating these little paper cases for the past three days, and they're not even chocolate." He held up some wrappers and then shoved them in his mouth. "You gotta help me, Mr. Slugworth, please. I got a taste for the brown stuff. I got it real bad."

Slugworth SCRUNCHED up his face, trying to swallow his disgust. He handed the Chief another box. "Here you go, Chief. And there's plenty more

where that came from. But stand down for now—
I'll give you a call when the time's right."

"Thank you, Mr. Slugworth," the Chief said.
"Thank you, thank you."

Slugworth lifted his binoculars and watched the
little girl help five suspiciously human-shaped
laundry bags down the chute.

"What is it, Arthur?" Fickelgruber asked.

"The girl," Slugworth said quietly.

"What girl?" Prodnose asked, grabbing the
binoculars. "Oh, *that* girl."

"You don't really think it could be . . . *her*, do
you?" Fickelgruber said.

"I do," Slugworth replied.

Fickelgruber became **FIDGETY**. "You
always assured us she wouldn't be a problem."

Prodnose nodded. "He's right; you did assure us."

"She won't be," Slugworth said coldly. "And
nor will Wonka. I'll see to it personally."

CHAPTER FIFTEEN

DOG

Mrs. Scrubitt wasn't used to visitors at night, and it was nearly midnight when a shadowy figure KNOCKED on her door.

She drew back the hatch, eyes roving around furiously as they sought out the person who had dared disturb her at such an hour.

"Who is it?" she growled. "What do you want?"

Slugworth stepped forward into the light of the hatch, his face menacing and cut through with shadows. "Mrs. Scrubitt?" he said, and there was a deathly silence. Then, suddenly, the door flung open!

"Mr. Slugworth!" Mrs. Scrubitt bellowed, falling over herself to let the man in.

Bleacher appeared behind her, a huge hulking presence emerging from the gloom. But as he got closer, Slugworth could see they were wearing sickly **SWEET** matching "his and hers" sets of pajamas, covered in knitted pictures of Tiddles.

"Who is it, my honey—WOW!" Bleacher cried. "It's the chocolatier himself!"

"To what do we owe this honor, sir?" Mrs. Scrubitt said with groveling courtesy.

"I wonder," Slugworth said, his lips curling into a mean smile, "if I might take a look in your washhouse?"

"What? Down to the suds? A strange request, especially at this time of night, but follow me," Bleacher grunted, leading the way down the stairs. Mrs. Scrubitt hurried along behind them.

"We're an item," she informed Slugworth

proudly. "Bavarian royalty, we are."

But Slugworth was barely listening. His fists were clenched and his pace was *QUICK*—he was clearly not in the mood for chitchat.

"I don't know what you're expecting to find down there," Mrs. Scrubitt rambled, her voice getting nervous. "It's just a perfectly normal washhouse serviced by a perfectly normal—"

She came to an abrupt halt and her mouth fell open when she saw it.

"Dog," she finished.

She and Bleacher stood in stunned silence as the full mechanized laundry powered entirely by Tiddles whirred and banged and popped in front of them.

"Tiddles," Bleacher said, shaking his head in dismay. "How could you?"

But that wasn't all. There was a mountain of strange jars, filled with ingredients that *SPARKLED* and **BUBBLED** and buzzed.

There was everything from thick globs of gunk to translucent liquids—some were fizzing and crackling wildly, while others were being neatly dispensed into cooking pans, one drip at a time.

Not a single one of the ingredients was identifiable.

"What in the name of worm water IS THIS?!" Mrs. Scrubitt cried.

"You have a guest—a Mr. Wonka," Slugworth said. "He's been sneaking out to sell chocolate with the help of your serving girl."

"That little brat!" Mrs. Scrubitt spat furiously.

Slugworth turned to Mrs. Scrubitt, a mean **GLINT** in his eye. "How would you like to help me put them out of business?" he said.

Mrs. Scrubitt eyed the potions and licked her lips greedily.

CHAPTER SIXTEEN

THE GRAND OPENING

For the washhouse workers, it had been nonstop building and painting and melting chocolate in secret. They had never been *HAPPIER*. And the best thing about it was Slugworth, Fickelgruber, and Prodnose were clearly completely unaware of what was going on in the Galeries Gourmet, right under their noses. Despite all the strange noises coming from behind the yellowing paper that lined the empty shop, no one came to ask any questions.

Soon the shop was ready, and the grand opening was upon them. Willy was a bonbon of nerves, a cream puff of fear, a big wobble of **JELLY-LIKE** excitement. He had scrubbed his purple coat for the occasion, and it had come up gleaming like new.

When the doors to the Galeries Gourmet opened, he was ready.

"Ladies and gentlemen!" he called, striking his cane to the ground. "Greetings to you all and welcome to Wonka's! Tremendous things are in store for you!"

An old man shuffling past stopped and stared up at him.

"What? In *there*?"

Willy turned and beamed up at his shop. *Wonka* was painted above the door in glistening gold, in the same style his mother had drawn on his birthday chocolate bar all those years ago. Inside, the place was **MYSTERIOUSLY** dark, the old chandelier still lying lifeless on the floor.

"Humor me," Willy said, holding out a hand for the old man. "Close your eyes and count to ten."

The old man reluctantly shut his eyes. "ONE . . ." he droned, and Willy led him into the darkened shop as he counted. ". . . NINE . . ." Then, very carefully, Willy lit a match and placed it in the chandelier.

"Make a wish!" Willy said. "Now open them!"

As the man did so, Larry yanked a rope and the chandelier shot upward! It swayed up high, illuminating all that was inside.

The man practically collapsed in shock when he saw the place. He grabbed Willy's arm to steady himself.

"Here's a store that's like no other. If it were, I wouldn't bother!" Willy chimed, and all around him was a whole landscape built entirely of chocolate and sweets! A lush green **MEADOW** of chocolate grass was peppered with chocolate

189

flowers and toadstools made of icing. In the center of the meadow sat a delicious-looking willow tree, its trunk carved from solid dark chocolate. Its branches hung low and dipped down into a chocolate river that flowed through the store.

"Chocolate trees, chocolate flowers," Willy said quietly, more to himself than the old man. "Memories made in chocolate that I won't let melt away again."

The old man suddenly gasped, because down the chocolate river came a chocolate barge boat, complete with a peppermint lining and filled with head-sized jelly beans!

Willy turned back to the door and saw someone walking toward him. The lights inside were blinding, making her no more than a silhouette, but she looked just like her. Hope **BUBBLED** up in his stomach, it was her—his mother was there, just like she said! But when she grew closer, he could see it was only a stranger with a young child skipping behind her.

"Welcome," Willy said as, with a sad smile, he snapped back to reality.

He picked a chocolate flower and gave it to the child. "It's all edible."

Soon, more and more customers were flocking to the shop as word spread that Willy was back. Before long, the place was packed to bursting with people screeching and shrieking and gasping at the edible world.

Willy skipped around the shop at speed, seizing customers' hands and shaking them vigorously. "Welcome, welcome!" he cried with excitement. He plucked flowers for them and scooped up cupfuls of melted chocolate from the river. "Here, try the river. It's *DELICIOUS*!" At one point he dived into a hole in the tree trunk and emerged at the top as he began climbing to the uppermost branches. The crowd applauded as he got all the way to the ceiling, where clumps of cotton-candy clouds floated. Then Willy raised his cane and pressed a button and the whole thing unfurled like an umbrella. Just in time, too—sweets started to fall like rain from above! The crowd went wild.

Then came the fireworks. But not any old ordinary fireworks. Willy's fireworks blasted across the sky, leaving *edible* strings in their wake! The customers grabbed for them, licking them and chewing them, their mouths so full their cheeks were ten times their normal size.

Willy watched the scene and felt a tingling sense of pride course through him.

A bubblegum balloon floated past, and he grabbed hold of it and soared through the air as the customers looked up at him in awe.

Over at the till, Noodle was packing up great

ARMFULS of chocolate. The old man was right at the front of the queue.

". . . and four dozen roses, and a bag of pears— ooh, and one of those clouds, please!" he said.

Abacus totted up his bill while Lottie passed him a cotton-candy cloud **FLOATING** on a string.

"Sir," Abacus said, looking up from his workings, "that comes to, er . . . nine hundred and eighty sovereigns."

"A bargain at twice the price!" the old man cried.

Noodle's jaw **DROPPED** as the man pressed ten notes into her hand.

"Wow, thank you, sir," she said. "Now, how do you want your change? Spendable or edible?"

"Ooh, edible, please!" the man said, and immediately the till dispensed some chocolate coins. He walked off with a spring in his step.

Noodle turned to Abacus, a huge grin on her face.

"Abacus," she said. "That customer just gave us a *thousand* sovereigns!"

"I know, Noodle! Isn't it fantastic?" Abacus said. "Now, who's next?"

But the old man only got as far as the door when something made him screech to a halt. "Er . . . Mr. Wonka?" he said.

Willy swiveled on his heel. "Yes, sir?"

The old man pulled off his hat and vivid purple hair spilled out. "My head feels **FUNNY**," he said.

Willy frowned. Noodle gasped! Not only was the man's hair purple, but each strand was multiplying at an alarming rate!

"Is my hair *growing*? It feels like it's growing," the old man said.

"Have you always had purple hair?" Willy asked.

The old man's eyes doubled in size. "WHAT?!" he cried. "NO!"

Willy began pacing, a mild panic now sizzling in his stomach. "It's not possible," he said, but then he stopped and looked down. "Unless . . ." he said, and he bent down and picked a flower. Carefully, he gave it the smallest of licks, and his heart sank. "Uh-oh," he said. "Yeti sweat!"

"**YETI SWEAT?!**" the old man cried, his hands moving to his new beard, which was growing so fast it had already reached the floor and was heading for the exit.

"The most powerful hair potion in the world," Willy explained. "Absolutely wonderful in the right conditions, but *I* didn't put it in here . . ." He turned to the room. "Ladies and gentlemen, there seems to be an error in the recipe. Please, nobody eat the flowers!"

Several customers looked up from the flower

beds, their faces smeared with chocolate. Multi-colored hair immediately started sprouting from their heads.

A man with luminous green hair popped up from the long grass. "But the pears are all right to eat, I presume?"

"Not the pears too?!" Willy cried.

"What's the matter with this licorice?" a woman roared. "My daughter had one bite, and just *look* at her!"

Willy watched as the child's mustache pinged and **CURLED** into ringlets.

"I like it!" her daughter shouted, holding each end of her new mustache defensively. "I SUIT IT!"

Willy raised his hands in the air to calm the crowd. "I'm terribly sorry, everyone. I don't know how this could have happened—but I regret to inform you that the chocolates have been . . . poisoned!"

"Poisoned?" a pink-haired customer squeaked.

"He poisoned my child!"

"I want my money back!"

Abacus started reluctantly handing the money back.

"I want compensation!"

"I want revenge!"

Someone hurled a chocolate pear at Willy, just missing him. It hit the wall and smashed into a thousand pieces. Willy stared down at it sadly.

The pear set the others off, and soon everyone was going *WILD*, jeering and flying around the room in a hairy rage. Chocolate was being launched in every direction and the woman with the mustached child was cutting through the rope that held the chandelier!

"Aaaaargh!" she cried in a fury, and the last threads of the rope snapped, sending the chandelier crashing to the ground. Willy watched in horror as the whole thing burst into flames!

"FIRE IN THE GALERIES GOURMET!" a customer roared.

Willy and the workers stood choking in the smoke as everyone else raced for the exit.

High up in their office above the arcade, Slugworth, Prodnose, and Fickelgruber stood at their office windows, smirking with **DELIGHT** as they watched Willy's dreams burn.

CHAPTER SEVENTEEN

POISON

When the fire had finally been extinguished and the firefighters had packed up and left, Willy stood in the charred remains, clutching his mother's chocolate bar.

The impressive chocolate tree had melted into a dripping blob, its **DELICIOUS** shine replaced with black blistering sores. The grass and flowers had been churned up and scorched, and the charred clouds were trampled into the floor. The barge boat had been smashed into pieces too, and Willy watched as each little bit of it sank down to the chocolaty depths.

"I don't understand," Lottie whispered. "What . . . what . . . ?"

"What happened?" Abacus finished for her.

"Isn't it obvious?" Piper said, her eyes **FLASH-ING** with fury. "The Chocolate Cartel."

"It's awful," Larry said. "I haven't been this sad since . . . Oh, I'm a clown; I'm sad all the time. Never mind."

Noodle put a hand on Willy's shoulder. "It's okay, Willy. We can rebuild. We can start again—"

"There's no point, Noodle," he interrupted. "It didn't work."

"It did! If the Chocolate Cartel hadn't meddled, then—"

"No, not that," Willy said, his eyes filling with tears. The words of his mother **ECHOED** in his mind. *And when you do share your chocolate with the world, I'll be right there beside you.* "She promised she would be here. And she wasn't."

"Your mother," Noodle said sadly, in a voice so small it was almost a whisper. "You didn't really think . . ." But she trailed off.

"I did think she would be here, Noodle," Willy said. "I really did. But it was just a stupid dream."

"Don't say that," Noodle said sternly. "You told me not to give up on my dreams; you can't give up on yours. You're Willy Wonka. You make impossible things happen! You can't . . . Don't ever—"

"Come on, everyone," Abacus said, gently leading Noodle away. "I think Mr. Wonka needs a moment to himself."

And so Willy stood alone, knee-deep in his broken dreams, watching the last of the barge disappear into the bubbling river. A single tear rolled down his cheek.

"Terrible shame what happened here," came a voice. Willy turned to see Slugworth marching in **TRIUMPHANTLY**. Trotting behind him were the other two.

"I take it you're responsible," Willy said. It felt as if Slugworth had sucked all the hope from him and he was back for the last dregs—like someone savoring the very last drops of a milkshake.

"Us?" Slugworth mocked. "No! Well, not personally. We may have 'encouraged' Mrs. Scrubitt to 'borrow' some of your ingredients and 'enhance' your creations."

"We paid her to poison them with some of your little potion bottles," Prodnose clarified.

"So why have you come?" Willy said. "To gloat?"

Slugworth **GRINNED**. "Oh no, Mr. Wonka. I don't waste my time with that sort of thing. We've come to offer you a deal."

Fickelgruber knelt down to open his suitcase. As he did so, Willy spotted three numbers penciled on the sole of his shoe. He handed Willy a wad of bank notes.

"This is the precise amount you owe Mrs. Scrubitt," he said, reaching back into his suitcase and producing more bundles of money. "This is for the number-cruncher, the plumber, the mousy one, the so-called funnyman . . ."

"By which he means not funny," Prodnose said.

"And the girl," Fickelgruber said, glancing at Prodnose impatiently before handing Willy a bigger bundle than all the others combined. "We've put in a bit extra for her. So she can get a place to live. Clothes. Toys. Books."

The mention of books made Willy look up. He remembered the first time he'd met her, the sound of the book snapping shut. Noodle loved books.

"You could change her life, Mr. Wonka," Slugworth said, weaving closer. "Change all their lives."

The thought that he still might be able to help his **FRIENDS** was enough to brighten his spirits a little. "What would I have to do?" he asked.

"Leave town," Slugworth said bluntly. "And never make chocolate again. There's a boat **SAILING** at midnight. And for the sake of your friends, and you, I hope you're on board."

Willy stared down at the money and knew he didn't have much of a choice. He would never have his dream or ever see his friends again. But they would be free—and Noodle, poor Noodle, would finally be happy.

CHAPTER EIGHTEEN

A ONE-WAY TICKET

When Willy arrived at the docks, the Chief and the Chocolate Cartel were there waiting for him.

"Your ticket, Mr. Wonka," Slugworth said with oily **CHARM**, brandishing a small handwritten ticket. "One way. To the North Pole."

"It's Premium Economy," Fickelgruber said.

"It's basically the same as Economy," Prodnose clarified. "But you get a bit more legroom and a fun-size packet of nuts."

The ship's horn sounded, and back in the city square, the clock chimed midnight.

"Now, I'd love to stay and chat, but, er . . . **TICK-TOCK**," Slugworth said impatiently, tapping his watch. Willy noticed that it had stopped at the wrong time again. "Goodbye, Mr. Wonka," Slugworth said, and he grabbed Willy's hand in a final bone-crushing handshake. Willy winced in pain as the man's ring cut into his flesh.

"Goodbye, Mr. Slugworth," Willy managed. He bowed his head in defeat and walked the gangplank.

On board, he handed his ticket to the waiting captain, who gave the Chief a sly nod, though Willy was too consumed with sadness to notice.

Within seconds of him boarding, the ship roared to life and was chugging out of the harbor toward the ocean. Willy didn't dare glance back. He couldn't.

Instead, he made his way to the front of the ship, where he found a wooden bench with a sign,

PREMIUM ECONOMY lazily scrawled on it. He settled into the seat and wrapped his plum coat around him. The sky was sleet gray and the snow was falling thick and fast now.

Then came a sound. A faint *clunk, clunk,* and scraping of wheels. Willy turned and was delighted to see the Oompa-Loompa lugging a tiny travel trunk behind him. He stopped at Willy's feet and opened it, revealing a **MINUSCULE** padded seat and minibar. He plucked an olive from a jar and held it up for Willy. "Olive?"

"I'm so glad you're here," Willy said, his voice cracking a little at the sight of a familiar face. "Really, I am."

"Oh, I'm not going to let you out of my sight, Willy Wonka," the Oompa-Loompa said. "Not until you've paid your debt. But I bring glad tidings on that score! I've been doing my sums. One more jar and we'll be even. Or, if you prefer,

I'll accept half a jar of those rather AMUSING Hoverchocs."

"Well, you're out of luck," Willy said, staring at the vast ocean ahead. "I don't make chocolate anymore."

"You don't mean you're going through with this ridiculous deal?" the Oompa-Loompa said.

"I have to. For Noodle," Willy said. "I promised her a better life. I pinkie promised."

"You should stand up to those bullies," the Oompa-Loompa said. "Give them the old one-two. That's what an Oompa-Loompa would do. But if you're determined to sit there feeling sorry for yourself, I'm going flat. Good night, sir."

Then he pressed a button and his chair started WHIRRING and began to recline. He released his finger from the button when it was completely flat and then pulled on an eye mask.

Willy shuffled uncomfortably in his hard seat.

His hand still ached from Slugworth's handshake. It was really throbbing. He held it up to take a better look.

"Huh," he said.

The Oompa-Loompa pressed the button on his chair again, and it whirred back to a seating position. He lifted his eye mask.

"What is it?" he asked.

"No, it's nothing," Willy said.

"It's not nothing, is it?" the Oompa-Loompa pressed. "You said *huh*."

Willy shook his head, his eyes still fixed on his hand. "Sorry. Forget it."

The Oompa-Loompa lowered his eye mask again.

"Huh!" Willy said again.

The Oompa-Loompa threw off his eye mask this time. "You did it again. And if you don't explain, I shall poke you viciously with a cocktail stick."

"Look where Slugworth shook my hand," Willy said, holding it out for the Oompa-Loompa to see. A red pattern was stamped on his skin. "His ring left a mark, see. An *A* surrounded by an *S*. Very **ORNATE**."

The Oompa-Loompa plucked a monocle from his pocket and held it up to take a good look. "So? His name is Arthur Slugworth," he concluded. "It's probably a family ring."

"But *Noodle* has one that looks just like it!" Willy said.

"Noodle?" the Oompa-Loompa said, and Willy nodded. "But why would the little orphan girl have a Slugworth family ring?"

"Only one reason I can think of," Willy said.

"Well, what is it?" the Oompa-Loompa asked.

"And if I'm right," Willy said, *SLOWLY* rising to his feet and staring off into the distance, "then she could be in great danger!" He began looking around frantically. "I've got to get back to land. Captain?!"

Willy shot off in search of the captain.

"We have to turn the ship around!" he cried. "Captain! Where are you? The ship! We need to turn it around!"

"Come back here!" the Oompa-Loompa shouted as he hurried after him. "I demand an explanation. What is your theory about the ring?!"

But Willy wasn't listening. He tore across the ship's bridge and came screeching to a halt at the wheelhouse. When he saw what was inside, a tingle of utter horror danced up his spine. There was no captain. But even worse than that, sitting in the captain's place was a **FIZZING**, furious BOMB!

"On second thought, the explanation can wait,"

the Oompa-Loompa said, and he inflated a tiny life jacket. "I do hope you can swim, Willy Wonka."

★★★

The Chief of Police stood with the three chocolatiers as they watched the ship skim the horizon.

Slugworth's lips mimed a countdown: "Five, four, three, two—"

BOOM!

And with that, every inch of the ship went hurtling off in all directions until the only thing left was a plume of smoke snaking up into the sky.

"Well, gentlemen," the Chief said. "One dead chocolatier, as requested."

Slugworth raised his walkie-talkie. "Miss Bon-Bon? Give the Chief his chocolate."

Miss Bon-Bon was not far behind them, manning a crane. She grabbed the controls and began lowering an **ENORMOUS** crate of chocolate down in front of the Chief. The chains clanged and the crane groaned as it swung dramatically in the wind above them. Miss Bon-Bon was sticking out her tongue in concentration as she poked at buttons. Then, all of a sudden, she swung the whole thing too far to the left! The chains *pinged* and **SNAPPED** and the chocolate landed on the Chief's car with an almighty *crunch*.

There was a groan of metal as the roof sagged, and then all four of the wheels popped off.

"And look, Miss Bon-Bon's loaded it into your car for you as well," Slugworth said as they all watched the wheels roll away.

The Chief didn't seem to care—because all he could see now was chocolate.

CHAPTER NINETEEN

★ SETTLING THE BILL

"My, my, what a lot of long faces we have this morning," Mrs. Scrubitt said cheerily as she **GREETED** the workers. They filed past her to the washhouse, but she put a leg out to stop them. "I've got some good news for you," she teased. "Not that you deserve it."

She placed a bundle of cash in the register and stamped Abacus's bill.

"Your friend Mr. Wonka's done a deal with Mr. Slugworth. Gave up his precious little dream to settle your accounts," she said. "So, Mr. Crunch, I believe you are free to go."

Abacus stood gawping at the inky *PAID* mark on the paper, completely frozen in shock.

"Mr. Crunch?" Mrs. Scrubitt said. "You're free to go."

"Go on!" Bleacher roared. "Scram!"

"Before I charge you for dawdlin'," Mrs. Scrubitt said with a **WAGGLE** of her finger.

Abacus took the receipt, flashed his fellow workers a delighted smile, and then shot off.

An excited murmur rippled through the group, but Noodle fixed the horrible woman with a stony stare. After a lifetime of being thrown in the coop, the generosity was . . . suspicious.

"Bell? Benz? Chucklesworth?" Mrs. Scrubitt droned as she ushered them out until only Noodle was left. She stood there, small and alone—the reality of just how alone she was began to sink in.

"Ah, Noodle," Mrs. Scrubitt said. "The biggest pile of the lot!" and much to Noodle's surprise, she plonked a heavy wad of cash down on the counter with a *BANG*.

Noodle's eyes grew **WIDE**, wider than they had ever grown before. She hadn't believed it was possible until that second, but there it was, her debt—and it was repaid. It was sitting right there, freedom and happiness and escape from the coop! Finally, she would be free; she could go and find Willy and the others!

Noodle reached out to touch it.

"Except this pile isn't to pay your bill, deary," Mrs. Scrubitt said, snatching it away.

"W-wait," Noodle stammered. "Then what—"

"It's to KEEP YOU HERE," Mrs. Scrubitt screeched with **GLEE**, and she began to laugh hysterically. She couldn't stop! She pounded the counter over and over again. Then she started dancing from foot to foot. "You thought you were leaving! Hah!"

Noodle stood frozen in shock as Bleacher bolted the door.

"My friend Mr. Slugworth doesn't think nasty little urchins like you should be out on the streets, not in a fine city like this!" Mrs. Scrubitt cackled. "He gave me this money to keep you down in the washhouse—for good!" She stopped laughing, and her face suddenly grew very serious. "And I am only too happy to oblige."

"I hate you!" Noodle screamed, charging for the window, but Bleacher grabbed her by the scruff of her neck and lifted her into the air.

"Look at her go, my lord," Mrs. Scrubitt said with a cruel smile.

"My lord?" Noodle said, and she began to **LAUGH**. "You don't still think he's *royalty*, do you?"

Mrs. Scrubitt looked confused.

"We made it all up, Mrs. Scrubitt," Noodle

shouted. "You worm-water-guzzling fool. He's not Bavarian royalty. He's not royalty at all!"

At that, Mrs. Scrubitt's face twisted in horror. First, she went as gray as her worm water, then she looked as if she might faint, then finally she turned a furious shade of purple, her veins popping in her head and her nostrils flaring.

"RIGHT! THAT'S IT!" she spat with more fury than Noodle had ever seen before. "YOU'RE GOING IN THE COOP, MY GIRL!"

She grabbed Noodle by the ear and dragged her out past Bleacher, who had momentarily forgotten he actually *wasn't* a German aristocrat and was completely floored by such a revelation.

"And take them dungarees off," Mrs. Scrubitt snapped at him, tears in her eyes. "You . . . you peasant!"

"**PUFFY-WUFF!**" Bleacher tried, but it was no good.

Mrs. Scrubitt dragged Noodle up the stairs and threw her into the coop, slamming the door so hard the pigeons panicked. Feathers went flying, claws snagged in Noodle's hair, and she screamed as the last of the birds fought their way out of the pigeonholes. She was alone once more.

A single tear rolled down her cheek, and she stared blankly ahead, wishing more than anything she hadn't dared to dream things might get better.

"Ah, there she is!" came a jarringly cheerful voice. "Hello, Noodle!"

She turned, and there was Willy, his face smooshed through one of the pigeonholes! She peeked out and saw he was balancing on a rickety ladder.

Noodle shook her head, convinced she was **DREAMING**.

"I . . . I thought you'd left," she said quietly. "I thought you'd all left me forever."

"I did," Willy explained. "I made a deal with the Cartel. Slugworth promised you a better life if I left forever, but he didn't *exactly* keep to his side of the bargain."

"No," Noodle said, her knees nestled in thick muck. "He didn't. In fact, the opposite—he wants me locked up forever, apparently."

"Of course he does," Willy mused as he produced a metal file and began cutting the padlock.

"Why?" Noodle asked. "What's he got against me? I've never even met him!"

"I don't know, Noodle, not for sure, but I think it might have something to do with your parents."

"My parents?" Noodle *WHISPERED*.

"It's just a theory," Willy said. "All I know for certain is you won't be safe until he's behind bars."

Abacus's face appeared in another of the pigeon-holes, making Noodle jump.

"Yes, how exactly is that supposed to happen, Mr. Wonka?" he asked.

"You said the Cartel keeps a record of all their dirty deeds?" Willy said, still going at the padlock.

Abacus nodded. "In the green ledger, yes."

"So if we could get ahold of that, we could prove they poisoned the chocolates. Scrubitt and Bleacher would go to jail and we'd all be free," said Willy.

"That sounds good to me," Piper said, her face appearing in the pigeonhole next to Willy.

"You're all here?" asked Noodle with a huge **GRIN**.

"Yes, of course, Noodle. We wouldn't leave you," Abacus said. "Now, Mr. Wonka, may I remind you that they keep the ledger in a vault?"

Lottie's face appeared in the pigeonhole next to Abacus.

"Guarded by a corrupt cleric," she said, flashing Noodle a smile.

"And five hundred chocoholic monks," Larry said, appearing next to Lottie.

"That's very true," Willy mused. "But I just had a long, cold swim. Cold water's very good for the brain—stimulates the neural pathways—and after just four miles, I figured out how an ingenious orphan, a plumber, a telephone-exchange operator, an accountant, and a man who can talk underwater could combine their skills and pull off a **MIRACLE**."

"Mr. Wonka," Abacus said, "it would be exceedingly complicated. Have you forgotten there's a code to get into the vault?"

"Yes, a nine-digit code, changes daily," Willy mumbled, his attention fixed on the padlock. He began hitting it. "I think I know where to find that code," he said.

"Really?!" Piper said. "Spit it out, then!"

"Well," Willy said, taking a break from whacking the padlock and **GLANCING** around to check no one could hear. He lowered his voice to a whisper. "When Prodnose's wig fell off in Galeries Gourmet, I noticed three numbers written on the inside. I didn't think anything of it at the time. But then last night, when Fickelgruber tried to bribe me, I saw he had three numbers written on the sole of his shoe. I'd bet anything that's where they keep their parts of the code!"

"You *might* be onto something," Piper said.

"That still leaves Slugworth," Noodle pointed out.

"You're not telling me he's daft enough to write down anything that important," Abacus said.

"He isn't," Willy said. "I noticed his watch was

broken the day I met him. I thought it was strange for a rich man to wear a broken watch. And it was still broken last night. But it told a *different time!*"

"Why would you change the time on a broken watch?" Lottie said slowly.

Noodle's eyes grew **WIDE**. "Because that's where he keeps his part of the code!"

"Exactly, Noodle!" Willy said as the padlock finally snapped and the coop sprung open.

"There's just one problem," Abacus said. "Even if you do get your hands on that ledger, the Cartel will simply buy their way out of trouble."

"It's the way of the world," Noodle said with a sigh.

"You're right, Noodle," Willy said. "I hate to admit it, but you are. That's why there's only one thing to do."

"What's that?" Noodle asked.

Willy's eyes **FLASHED** with mischief. "Change the world."

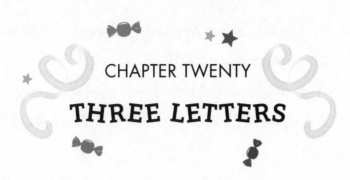

CHAPTER TWENTY

THREE LETTERS

A delivery boy cycled through the city streets with a lumpy sack full of letters. On top of the pile sat three very **SPECIAL** letters indeed.

The first one was for Arthur Slugworth, and when the boy screeched to a halt outside the Galeries Gourmet, he rushed immediately to Slugworth's office and handed it to Miss Bon-Bon. Her eyes practically popped out of their sockets when she saw the stamp on it, and she ran as fast as she could, bursting through Slugworth's door.

"Miss Bon-Bon!" he cried. "Don't you know how to knock?!"

He was lying face down on a massage table as a masseuse pummeled his back.

Miss Bon-Bon held the letter below his face. It was stamped with a gold and **ENTICINGLY** swirly *W*.

He leaped up and tore open the letter angrily, his eyes darting back and forth as he devoured the letter with furious speed.

Dear Mr. Slugworth,
Last night you offered me a deal that I have decided to decline.

I am, however, prepared to offer you a new deal. I will work for you and you alone. With your nose for business and my talent, we could bankrupt the other two members of your so-called cartel and split the profits two ways instead of three.

Farther up the street, the delivery boy was

already at his next drop-off stop: the tailor's. He plucked the letter from the pile, folded the edges over, shaping it into a paper airplane. Then, with impressive precision, he lobbed it through the window of the tailor's. It hit Fickelgruber square on the nose.

"I'm being fitted for a suit, you peasant!" Fickelgruber cried out to the boy. He made to throw away the letter, but something caught his eye. A *GLINTING* gold *W.*

The message inside, though he didn't know it, was identical to the one Slugworth had received.

I will work for you and you alone . . .

The final letter was for Prodnose, but when the delivery boy arrived at his residence, there was no answer at the door. He paused, looking for an open window to throw it into, but when he realized there wasn't one, he squashed the letter into a ball and gave it a big kick so it sailed up to the roof and straight down the chimney! It fell perfectly, landing in the fireplace in the top floor bathroom, where Prodnose happened to be **LUXURIATING** in an afternoon bubble bath.

He reached out a soapy hand and grabbed the letter.

I will work for you and you alone . . .

"Well, I like the sound of that!" Prodnose said.

If you wish to discuss terms, go to Heimlich's Newsstand at 8:15.

But this is where the letters were different. Although Prodnose was instructed to go to the newsstand, Fickelgruber was told to head to the shoeshine stall, and Slugworth to the old school.

All at once, Prodnose leaped from his bath, Fickelgruber pushed away his tailor, and Slugworth called for his butler.

"Tell Donovan to bring the car!"

***

In the zoo security hut, the guard lay sleeping, having just consumed another Party Choc.

"**UNBELIEVABLE**," Abacus said as he stood over the unconscious man.

"Isn't it?" Willy mused. He grabbed the keys to the truck, and the two of them hurried into the zoo and found Abigail.

"It's a giraffe, Willy!" Abacus cried. "We're collecting A GIRAFFE?"

"Morning, Abigail," Willy said. "How'd you like to earn a few more acacia mints?" He gestured at the rickety zoo van parked by the entrance. "It will involve a little jaunt *outside* your enclosure, but I assure you it is quite safe. Nothing more than a mere caper."

Across town, Lottie sneaked into the telephone exchange and waited. Meanwhile, Noodle had donned a shawl and was running after the priest. She hurried up to him and tugged at his coat.

"Couldn't spare a piece of chocolate for a starvin' orphan, could ya?" she rasped as she **SURREPTITIOUSLY** slipped something into his pocket.

"I'm sorry, my child, I don't have any chocolate on me," the priest said.

"NEVER MIND!" Noodle cried, and much to the priest's astonishment, the strange girl skipped off down the street as if something **WONDERFUL** had just happened! He didn't know what to make of this unusual scene, but that's because he hadn't looked in his pocket . . .

CHAPTER TWENTY-ONE

UNCOVERING
THE CODE

Prodnose arrived promptly at the newsstand, his eyes greedily scanning the crowd for Willy. He was so engrossed in his search, he didn't notice the clown **LUMBERING** up behind him with a large horn.

"Here we go," Larry whispered nervously. He honked the horn as loudly as he could—but the nerves got the better of him and rather than a honk or two he just kept going! *HONK, HONK, HONK, HONK, HONK, HONK.*

Prodnose swung around and as he did so Larry gave another big *HOOOONK*, and it produced a blast of air so strong it knocked Prodnose's wig clean off.

"Oi!" Prodnose cried. "What do you think you're doing?"

He bent down to pick up his hair, but Larry got there first and shot off with it around the corner.

"Come back here with my cat—I mean hair!" Prodnose screamed and he shot off after him.

Larry stopped and thumbed the wig, his hands shaking. Inside, just as Willy had said, he found the numbers they needed: 642. He **MEMO-RIZED** them and then turned back to Prodnose.

"Hey, pal," Larry said, "get a leash on that thing!"

Prodnose tried to snatch the wig back, but Larry held on to it and whispered, "Willy Wonka says to meet him at the old copper mine." Then he melted into the crowd.

Not far away, Fickelgruber arrived at the shoeshine stall and looked around expectantly. His nose wrinkled in disgust at the sight of the grubby people on their knees **SHINING** shoes.

Piper looked up and flashed him a smile. "Shoe-shine, mister?"

Fickelgruber nodded and sat on the steps, his eyes on the crowd as he looked for Willy. "You haven't seen a man dressed in a plum tailcoat, have you?" he asked Piper.

"No, sir," she said, lifting his shoe and making a note of the numbers on the sole: 273. Then she dropped the polish, rose to her feet, and whispered, "Willy Wonka says to meet him at the old copper mine."

And before Fickelgruber could say anything, she darted off.

Finally, Slugworth was at the school as

instructed. He stood inside, still and steely, like the statue of a great god.

Larry approached immediately, **CONFIDENT** from his last encounter with a chocolatier, and grabbed his hand.

"Is that . . . the incredibly famous Mr. Slugworth?! I want one of those bone-crushing business handshakes everyone talks about!" Larry chuckled as his eyes searched Slugworth's wrist for the watch.

"Get off!" Slugworth shouted, snatching his hand back.

Larry began to sweat. There was no watch.

"Something the matter?" Slugworth said.

"Uh . . . no," Larry said. "I just wondered if I could shake your other hand?" He grabbed Slugworth's other hand. There was no watch there either!

"Get lost!" Slugworth shouted, pushing Larry away.

"Willy Wonka says to meet him at the old copper mine," Larry shouted in a panic as he scuttled off. He stumbled outside and bumped into Piper.

"Get it?" Piper asked **HOPEFULLY**.

"No!" Larry panted.

"What do you mean, 'no'?" Piper cried.

Larry collapsed in a worried heap. "He wasn't wearing a watch!"

Piper spied Slugworth storming out of the school, tucking a watch into his pocket.

"He's got it on a chain! He has a pocket watch today!" she cried. "Look!"

Larry slapped a hand to his forehead. "Just my LUCK! What are we going to do?"

Without a second thought, Piper charged off toward the chocolatier and ran straight into him. He slipped and skidded and spread his arms to steady himself.

"What are you doing, you damn fool?!" he bellowed, shoving her out of the way. He took one last look at the crowd and, accepting Willy wasn't there, climbed back into his car and sped off.

"Well . . ." Larry whispered as he sneaked over. "Did you get it?"

Piper held up the pocket watch and smiled smugly. She noted the time: 8:16.

CHAPTER TWENTY-TWO

ABIGAIL IS
ON THE LOOSE

The priest stepped outside the cathedral and froze. Then he rubbed his eyes in disbelief. Standing in the middle of the street and eyeing him with a great hunger was a *giraffe*!

Unfortunately, rubbing his eyes meant he momentarily broke eye contact, and that just **EMBOLDENED** Abigail to move closer.

She raised her nose in the air and sniffed.

"There, there. Steady. Nice giraffe," the priest said nervously, starting to back up. Well, Abigail didn't like that. She began striking her hoof against the ground.

The priest was sweating now, his entire body wobbling in fear. Even his face and cheeks were **WOBBLING** like a crème caramel.

"Save yourselves!" he screamed as he fell back into the cathedral and slammed the doors shut. He tore down the aisle, past worshippers in quiet prayer and a few very confused monks. "Get up! Quick! It's a . . . It's the—the . . . NECK ONE!" He was so agitated, he'd forgotten the word "giraffe." Then Abigail crashed through the doors and galloped down the aisle behind him. The congregation exploded into panic. Stuff was flying everywhere—bags, shoes, hats—and everyone was screaming as the sound of thundering hooves rose up into the rafters. The priest stumbled up the steps and into the pulpit and grabbed a telephone that was hidden beneath the lectern.

"What have I done to deserve this?" he whimpered to himself as he punched in the numbers.

You know what you've done, Julius. Sold your soul for twenty pieces of chocolate! "Operator? Operator!"

"Hello, operator!" came Lottie's voice. "How may I direct your call?"

"I need the zoo! It's an emergency!" the priest said.

"Putting you through now," Lottie said confidently. "Stand by, caller!"

There was a click, and in a telephone box nearby, the phone rang.

Larry **CRACKED** his knuckles and then picked up the receiver, while Willy, Noodle, Abacus, and Piper stood around him, looking at each other nervously.

"Hello, zoo?" Larry lied.

The rest of the group made animal noises.

"Quiet down, you animals," Larry said, trying not to laugh. "You too, octopus," he added, putting on an underwater voice.

"HAVE YOU LOST A GIRAFFE?" the priest screamed.

"Oh yeah, I think we did lose a giraffe," Larry said. "Well, it's easy to do, isn't it?"

The others could hear the priest's exasperated shouts down the phone.

"Yes, easy to lose, that's what I said," Larry said, his voice cracking with laughter.

The priest's shouts became **HIGH-PITCHED** now.

"Okay, okay!" Larry said. "I'll send the team round to pick up the giraffe. You just sit tight."

Back at the cathedral, the priest hung up the phone and breathed a sigh of relief. But it was short-lived—he felt a gust of warm breath on his neck. Slowly he turned to see two huge, hungry eyes peering down at him. Abigail began sniffing and the priest began to whimper. She sniffed his face and his neck, her muzzle whiskers scratching at his throat and making him wince. Then suddenly, she plunged her head down into his pocket! A crunching sound made the priest jolt in surprise. When he looked down, he couldn't believe his eyes. His pocket was full of **BRIGHT** green knobbly sweets! By some awful miracle, his pockets had been filled with mints! Mints now being demolished by an overenthusiastic giraffe!

He was thrown from side to side as Abigail tried to wriggle her nose farther down into his pocket. He strained and spun, pulling his arms free of his robe, which collapsed to the ground as he vaulted over the pulpit to safety.

Then suddenly a *beep* sounded outside and the zoo truck burst through the doors, **WEAV-ING** around the debris from the fleeing congregation and screeching to a stop in the middle of the cathedral.

Abacus, Piper, and Larry jumped out.

"Better if you leave now," Abacus said to the priest. "It's safer."

The priest didn't need to be told twice. He ran as fast as he could, out of the cathedral doors, and didn't look back.

Willy sat huddled in the back of the van, covered in straw that smelled of wet giraffe. Noodle was next to him, sitting with her legs tucked up to her chin and breathing only from her mouth to avoid the smell. A nervous EXCITEMENT bubbled in Willy's stomach at the thought of the plan coming together.

Piper hauled the door open. "Coast is clear," she said. "Come on!"

Willy and Noodle burst from the straw and made for the confessional. Willy squeezed inside first, while Abacus took the priest's side. Piper handed Noodle the codes and she squeezed in too—there was barely enough room for the two of them.

No one was saying anything as a catching nervousness spread through the group. Abacus gave Willy a **SUPPORTIVE** nod, and then he pulled the lever. A whirring sounded and the confessional booth began to shake and shift, and soon it was descending into the depths below.

"Here we go," Willy whispered as they sank down into darkness.

CHAPTER TWENTY-THREE

FLAMINGO JAM

*P**ing!* As the elevator doors opened into the crypt, the security chief looked up with surprise to see not a guest but a box of chocolates, wrapped with a ribbon and placed neatly on a stand.

She stepped inside the elevator and plucked the accompanying card from the stand.

Thank you for all your hard work. Please enjoy these chocolates from us.

—Father Julius and the Chocolate Cartel

"Oh, that's sweet," she said, unwrapping one

of the chocolates and shoving it in her mouth. Almost immediately, she was dribbling and slurping and **BOUNCING** off the ceiling.

"Is she now *crying*?" Noodle asked from their hiding place above the elevator.

"And finally . . ." Willy said. He flicked his hand. *Thud*. "PARTIED OUT."

Meanwhile, across town, Slugworth's limousine nosed its way slowly through a flock of flamingos blocking the road.

"Sorry about this, sir," Slugworth's driver said. "But a prawn-delivery van crashed and spilled everywhere, and you know how flamingos are."

"Well, hurry it along, will you?" Slugworth said. "Tick-tock, tick-tock."

He reached for his pocket watch and jolted in shock when his hand could find nothing but . . . pocket!

The vein in his forehead began bulging, his

furious eyes moving back and forth as he sifted through his recent memory.

"That woman!" he shouted suddenly, remembering his collision with Piper. He reached for his car phone and dialed.

"Father. Everything all right there?" he asked urgently.

"Oh yes, Mr. Slugworth. All is **WELL**," the priest said. "At least it is now!"

"What do you mean, 'it is *now*'?" Slugworth pressed.

"Oh, we had a giraffe in here earlier," the priest said.

Slugworth turned to see a flamingo aggressively pecking at his window. "Sorry the line is bad—A what? It sounded like you said 'giraffe,' but that can't be ri—"

"Yes!" the priest interrupted. "A giraffe! From the zoo! We had to clear the whole place for about twenty minutes, but everything's back to normal now."

Slugworth hung up and dialed Fickelgruber and Prodnose on his special cartel phone. It was a direct line to every member all at the same time.

"Gentlemen," Slugworth said, "where are you?"

"On my way to see the tailor," Fickelgruber lied.

"I'm . . . just having a bath," Prodnose screeched. "I am!"

The line fell **SILENT** before Slugworth said faintly, "In your car?"

"It's . . . a car bath?" Prodnose squeaked. "Why, haven't you got one?"

Slugworth sat very still as he listened down the line. Pecking on windows . . . The same squawks and **FLAPPING** sounds . . .

"Hello?" Fickelgruber and Prodnose said at once.

"I'm still here," Slugworth said. "And so are

you—we're stuck in a flamingo jam. You're going to see Wonka. We all are. Except he's not going to be there."

"Why? Where is he?" Fickelgruber asked.

"In the crypt," Slugworth said, a red rage consuming him. *"Robbing us."*

CHAPTER TWENTY-FOUR

THE VAULT AND THE TRUTH

Willy and Noodle stood by the **GAR- GANTUAN** steel door to the vault. There were three individual coded dials, one marked for each chocolatier.

Noodle held up the three pieces of paper from Piper. She read them out slowly and carefully so Willy wouldn't make a mistake.

"Six, four, two," she said. "Two, seven, three, nine, one, eight."

Willy dialed in the combination, took a deep breath, and then together they heaved the huge wheel dial, trying to open it.

"One, two . . ." Willy whispered. "Th—"

The lock didn't budge.

"It's the wrong code!" Noodle cried. "It didn't work!"

Willy slumped. They were inches away from the final piece of their plan, but without the code, they might as well have been all the way back at the start.

"Ah!" Noodle said, making Willy **JUMP**. "Hang on a minute . . ."

"What is it, Noodle?" he asked hopefully, and then he saw what she was doing. She was rotating the last piece of paper.

"It might've been upside down," she said. "Try eight, one, six."

CLUNK!

"Noodle!" Willy cried, looking at her in **AWE** as he heaved the heavy door open to reveal a secret lair filled with pipes and valves and strange controls and clanging machinery. "Well done. You passed the test."

"What test?" Noodle asked.

"The upside-down number test," Willy replied.

"That's not a test."

"It absolutely is a test. Now," he said, his eyes scanning the room. "Let's find that ledger."

They raced into the lair, emptying drawers and upending piles of paper. They searched under chairs and under rugs. They searched everywhere.

"Anything?" Willy asked.

Noodle threw some chocolate boxes to the ground in frustration. "Nothing!"

"Well, keep looking," Willy said. "It's here; it must be."

Noodle slumped into a chair. "It's not here, Willy."

"It must be. Abacus told us—"

"Abacus has been in the washhouse for the past four years," Noodle said. "Maybe they changed it.

Maybe all that scrubbing went to his head. All that's down here is a load of stupid old chocolate!" She picked up a box of Slugworth's chocolates and threw them hard. The chocolates went **FLYING** across the room, the box crashed into a tile on the wall, and a strange *click* sounded. Then the tile did an incredible thing. It flipped open to reveal a hidden compartment behind it!

Inside was a **CHUNKY** book bound in green leather.

"The green ledger!" Willy cheered, grabbing it and hoisting it in the air. "You had me going there for a minute, Noodle. But you knew where it was all along!"

"No, I didn't. I just—"

Suddenly there was a *BANG*. Willy turned to see Slugworth armed and blocking their only exit. Fickelgruber and Prodnose stood smugly by his side.

"Naughty, naughty, Mr. Wonka," Slugworth snarled. "You've caused us quite a bit of trouble, you and your urchin."

"She's not just an urchin, though, is she?" Willy said, bravely stepping forward, eager not to miss his chance to find some answers. "You're family."

"What?" Noodle said. "What are you talking about, Willy?"

"You know that ring?" he said gently. "The one you got from your parents? Well, Mr. Slugworth has one just like it. Don't you, Mr. Slugworth?"

Slugworth **NARROWED** his eyes at Willy as Noodle pulled the ring from around her neck.

"That was my brother's ring," Slugworth said, his eyes still fixed on Willy. "Zebedee, he was called."

Noodle stared down at the necklace and whispered. "Was he my father?"

"A hopeless romantic is what he was!" Slugworth spat. "Fell in love with a common little bookworm but died before they could marry, leaving me sole heir to the family fortune. Or so I thought. Then I heard *you* were soon to be born, another heir with a claim to *my* money. But as **LUCK** would have it, not long after you arrived, your mother showed up on my doorstep, begging me to get a doctor for her sick little newborn . . . I said to leave the child with me—I could help."

Willy moved closer to Noodle, worried for his friend. The news didn't seem to have sunk in—she remained emotionless, her face blank and unreadable. But then the hand gripping her ring began to shake.

"Of course, I had other plans," Slugworth said with a wicked grin.

"You didn't take me to a doctor," Noodle said. "You took me to Scrubitt and Bleacher."

"Down the laundry chute you went!" Slug-worth laughed. "To a sad little life!"

"Not *N* for Noodle," she said as she thumbed the ring. "*Z* for Zebedee."

"It's the meanest story I've ever heard!" Willy cried in disbelief. "And what lie did you tell her mother to cover your tracks?"

"Oh, I said the baby had died," Slugworth said dismissively. "I gave her a bag of sovereigns and sent her back where she came from. She was heartbroken, but she believed me."

Willy turned his attention to the beefy green ledger, **FLICKING** through as fast as he could go.

"Where did you send her back to, Slugworth?" Noodle said, her voice desperate. "She might be out there still! What's her name?"

"Ooh," Slugworth said, tapping his chin. "Now then, what was it . . . ? Umm . . . No, I don't think

I can remember that. You must understand, she was very poor."

Fickelgruber retched at the word.

"Sorry, Felix," Slugworth said.

Willy stopped rifling through the pages of the ledger and looked up, his stomach **FLIP-FLOPPING**. "I've found her," he said. "Noodle, she was called Dorothy Smith."

Noodle stared at Willy in disbelief. "You found her?"

"Look," Willy said, pointing to an entry in the ledger. "She's right here."

Noodle read the ledger, then suddenly her head snapped up. "Wait, Willy, how did you read that?"

"I guess you did teach me to read after all," he said with a smile.

"Well, this is all very touching," Slugworth said. "But I've got a treat for you."

Fickelgruber snatched the ledger from Willy.

"What treat?" Noodle asked.

Slugworth fixed her with a grim **GRIN**.

"DEATH BY CHOCOLATE!" he snarled.

CHAPTER TWENTY-FIVE

DEATH BY CHOCOLATE

The Cartel marched Noodle and Willy through a steel door with a small porthole window at the far end of the lair. Inside, an enormous tank filled with chocolate bubbled before them, looking like a great big—and very deadly— **MIXING** bowl. Whirring blades sliced angrily through the mixture.

Fickelgruber pulled a lever, and to Willy's relief, the blades stopped. But his relief was short-lived.

"On you go," Slugworth said, nudging the pair on to the top of the blade that stretched out before them. He gestured along the blade all the way to the middle of the tanks where a small metal island sat—the steel plate that held the blades in place.

"Considering the situation," Willy said as they made their way to the center of the tank, "I wondered if you gentlemen would do a good deed on my behalf?"

"A what?" Fickelgruber spat.

"A good deed," Prodnose clarified for him. "It's a sort of pointless act of selflessness."

"Of course, Mr. Wonka," Slugworth said **QUICKLY**, clearly keen to move things along. "What is it you want us to do?"

Willy reached into his hat and pulled out a jar of chocolates.

"I wonder if you could give these to someone— only if you happen to see him, you understand." Willy tossed the chocolates back to the Cartel.

"Who is it?" Slugworth asked.

"A little orange man, about this high." Willy

held his hand to his knee. "And he has green hair."

"Eh?" Slugworth said.

"I owe him a jar of chocolates," Willy said. "And, well, I think these might be the best I've ever made."

He **JIGGLED** the jar. Inside were Hoverchoc-shaped chocolates, only these ones were striped in vivid shades of purple, green, and blue.

"Right. Sure, I'll see he gets them," Slugworth said dismissively. *"Now keep walking."*

Willy and Noodle had no choice. They inched their way across the perilous blade to the little island. Fickelgruber pulled the lever once more, and the huge blade started up again, trapping them there.

Willy and Noodle watched in horror as the chocolatiers then left the room, sealing the door behind them. Beyond the porthole the men stood at a wall of valves in the lair, turning them one by one. Immediately, chocolate came bursting from three pipes that lined the tank, spilling down like

THUNDERING waterfalls—one from each chocolatier's factory. The level rose fast, and soon the liquid was splashing against their shoes.

Willy gulped. In seconds they were lifted up by the liquid, rising toward the roof of the tank. But the force of the blade was pulling them down, deeper into the chocolate.

They watched hopelessly as the chocolatiers retreated farther back into the lair, and could see Fickelgruber returning the ledger to the secret compartment.

"Willy!" Noodle shouted as the chocolate reached their stomachs. "Start kicking. We have to stay afloat."

She was right: if the blade dragged them under, they'd be churned to pieces. But the roof of the tank was inching closer, and once they reached the top, they'd surely drown.

But Willy had other concerns on his mind.

He began pulling bottles of ingredients from his pockets and chucking them **HAPHAZ-ARDLY** into the mixture.

"What are you doing?" Noodle cried.

"If we're going to die in chocolate, Noodle," he said, "then it's going to be Wonka chocolate."

★★★

PING! The elevator arrived back up in the cathedral and the Cartel stepped out. Slugworth looked at the jar of Wonka's chocolates.

"Best he's ever made, eh?" And then he grabbed a handful and put them in his mouth. The others did the same.

"Now, um, gentlemen," the priest said sheepishly as he appeared behind them. "It was a bit of a close shave today, and I was wondering if we should rethink our arrangement or . . ."

Slugworth threw him the jar with the last of the chocolates, and the man's face lit up.

"Or just leave things as they are!" the priest said, licking his lips.

"That Wonka might have been as **NUTTY** as a fruitcake," Slugworth said as the Cartel made for the door, "but he sure knew how to make chocolate."

"Do you think we should have saved some for the small orange man with the green hair?" Prodnose asked.

"Tell me you're joking," Fickelgruber said.

"Of course I am!" Prodnose cried before asking, "Why am I joking?"

"Because there's no such thing, you nincompoop!" Slugworth bellowed.

"I knew that!" Prodnose said indignantly. "But then, why did he say there was . . . ?"

★★★

Back in the tank, Willy's and Noodle's heads were bobbing perilously close to the ceiling of the tank. The chocolate was **SLOSHING** into their mouths, and Willy knew it was only seconds before their entire heads would go under. Up above them, they spotted a small, round window.

"Help! Help! Help!" they screamed over and over again, desperately banging on the glass. Suddenly shadows floated over them.

"People!" Noodle said, spluttering chocolate. "It's the cathedral up there. They heard us!"

But then the shadows grew closer, and their faces became clear.

"Oh, not *them*," Willy cried as Slugworth, Fickelgruber, and Prodnose grinned down at the pair. Those smug **SMILES** were the last thing Willy and Noodle saw before the chocolate flooded their faces and the world disappeared.

CHAPTER TWENTY-SIX

OOMPA-LOOMPA IN AN ELEVATOR

The priest sat huddled in the confessional, polishing off the last of the chocolates, muttering guiltily to himself.

"You must pull yourself together," he whispered. "**HONESTLY**, stop worrying about these very minor misdeeds; it's not like anyone is going to appear and punish you. It's just chocolate."

"Correction," came a growl, and the priest looked down to where the noise came from, right next to his shoes.

"It's *my* chocolate," the Oompa-Loompa said. "Imagine my SURPRISE when I followed the smell and it led me to *you*. EATING MY CHOCOLATES!"

The priest immediately fainted, and the empty jar dropped into the Oompa-Loompa's arms. His face grew very serious indeed.

"You steal from an Oompa-Loompa, we take back a thousandfold!" he bellowed, then he stopped and sniffed the air. Chocolate, lots of it . . . He sniffed again. Underground! The perfect compensation. He spotted the little lever next to the priest and pulled it down. Much to his surprise, the confessional box began to move . . .

When the elevator door opened in the crypt, the Oompa-Loompa pulled a string by his side, and a pair of mechanical wings unfurled from his jacket. He took off, soaring through the vault, following his nose all the way to the chocolate tank. He hovered at the small porthole window and watched the churning chocolate. But then something shocking caught his eye—a familiar top hat **SWIRLING** in the mixture. He gasped when he realized, and quick as a flash, he darted to the wall of valves and controls where he spotted a lever marked EMERGENCY DRAIN. He pulled it, and immediately the tank started glugging and bubbling, and much to the Oompa-Loompa's delight, the blades stopped churning and the level began to fall. The Oompa-Loompa bit his nails, wincing as he waited to see what would be left of Willy at the end of it.

Inch by inch, the chocolate slopped out of the tank. It was so quiet, so still, so lifeless down there.

Then suddenly, Willy and Noodle broke the surface, coughing and spluttering and taking enormous gulps of air.

"We're alive!" Noodle cried with joy, giving Willy a hug before shaking some chocolate out of her ear.

Willy could hardly believe it. He was so happy he began doing somersaults, swirling around and around in the vortex of chocolate as it drained from the tank. Soon it was almost empty, with only some chocolate puddles remaining at the bottom.

"We've been **SAVED!**" Noodle said, splashing about happily in what little chocolate remained. "Who saved us?"

Willy glanced up and spotted a small figure hovering by the window.

"Aha!" he said, giving his friend a **GRATE-FUL** nod. "It was the little orange man with the green hair, Noodle."

"I'm serious, Willy," Noodle said.

"So am I!" Willy said. "He's right there."

But when Noodle looked up, the Oompa-Loompa was gone.

CHAPTER TWENTY-SEVEN

THE EMPTY JAR

The Cartel emerged from the cathedral just as the Chief lumbered around the corner, accompanied by Affable and a couple of assisting officers. Eating 1,800 boxes of chocolates had really taken its toll. His face was gray and smeared with chocolate; his eyes were as heavy-looking as his stride. He **PUFFED** to a halt, and cried, "Gentlemen! Thank goodness you're all right! I came as fast as I could. A robbery, you say?"

"Don't you worry, Chief. Everything's under control. Couple of thieves broke in, but I'm afraid they met with a little accident," Slugworth said grimly.

"In which they died," Prodnose clarified.

The Cartel all laughed.

"What's the big **JOKE**?" came a voice, and they all turned in horror to see Willy standing on the cathedral steps with Noodle, dripping in chocolate and very much alive.

"Wonka!" Slugworth bellowed. "You should be dea—" He stopped when he saw what was in Noodle's hand, and then he started to tremble.

"Officer," Willy said, calling to Officer Affable. "Would you kindly take a look at this?"

Noodle handed him the green ledger.

"It details every single illegal payment these men have ever made," Noodle explained, flashing the Cartel a satisfied smile. "Thousands of them."

Behind them, the priest sidled out of sight.

"Don't listen to her, Affable," the Chief cried. "She's lying!"

"Well, of course she is!" Slugworth spat.

Officer Affable opened the ledger, and his eyes grew wide as he leafed through the pages. "She's not, sir," he said. "She's absolutely right. It's . . . **INCREDIBLE**."

Sweat began to form on the Chief's brow. He went for a different approach. "Oh. Well. Then it sounds like a case for the Chief of Police. Give it to me, Affable. I'll take it from here."

But as the Chief grabbed for the ledger, Officer Affable held on tightly.

"I can't let you have it, I'm afraid, sir," he said.

"And why's that?" the Chief asked as he glanced nervously at Slugworth.

"Your name's in here too, Chief," Officer Affable said. "A lot."

The Chief dropped to his knees. "Curse my **SWEET** tooth!" he squealed.

It was as good a confession as any, and with a nod from Officer Affable, the other officers moved in to arrest the Cartel and the Chief.

"All right, I'll confess. I'm weak. I'll flip," the Chief wailed. "I'll name names. I mean, you know their names, but I'll name them anyway. All I ask is just a little bit of chocolate . . ."

"Gentlemen?" Slugworth said, sensing the game was up. "Run!"

They shot off through the square, but before they could get far, something incredible happened. Their feet lifted off the ground, and they soared up into the sky!

"Oh no! Not again!" Slugworth wailed.

"You didn't eat any of those chocolates, did you, Mr. Slugworth?" Willy called up to them as they rose **HIGHER** and **HIGHER**.

Slugworth bared his teeth in fury. "Why?"

"Because they're Hoverchocs," Willy shouted. "My new delayed-action version. And extra strong. At the speed you're going, I'd say the three of you ate the lot!"

Slugworth grabbed hold of a jet of frozen water sticking out of the fountain, then Fickelgruber grabbed Slugworth's shoe and Prodnose grabbed Fickelgruber's ankle. There they were: the formidable Chocolate Cartel, a neat little string of criminal bunting in the sky.

"You think you're so **CLEVER**, don't you?" Slugworth shouted down to Willy. "Well, there's a billion sovereigns of chocolate beneath our feet. We'll get the best lawyers, bribe the judge, rig the jury if we have to. We'll be *fine*."

"I wish I'd thought of that," Willy said, a hint of a smile breaking on his face. "Noodle?"

Noodle gave a nod and clanged a wrench

against the fire hydrant. It was the final part of the plan, the bit they had all been looking forward to. Deep below, huddled among the city's pipework, the others heard her signal.

"Now!" Piper cried, and together she, Abacus, Lottie, and Larry began unscrewing bolts on the pipes.

"What are you doing, Wonka?" Slugworth shouted down, his voice ripe with suspicion. "Why did she clang that fire hydrant?"

Noodle just smiled sweetly up at him as the ground beneath their feet began to quake. Tiles slipped from rooftops, the melons rolled off the fruit cart, and everyone in the square stopped and looked down.

The icicles on the fountain's spouts began to creak and crack. Slugworth's hand slipped slightly as he tried to cling TIGHTER on to his icicle. Then suddenly there came the sound of rushing water and the fountain burst back to life! Only, it wasn't water.

"It's chocolate!" Slugworth screamed.

Prodnose gasped. "Our chocolate!"

"We're ruined!" Fickelgruber cried.

Immediately, the icicle Slugworth was holding snapped in two, and the chocolatiers floated up and away.

"Ruined?" Willy called to them. "I don't know—to me it looks like you're going up in the world!"

"By which he means we're physically going up," Prodnose clarified. "But financially—"

"Oh, shut up, Prodnose!" Slugworth shouted.

"You're an idiot!" Fickelgruber added.

"Well, at least I'm not sick every time someone mentions the poor," Prodnose scoffed, and they began grabbing at each other, kicking and throwing punches as they drifted higher and higher into the sky. But only Willy was watching them; everyone else was fixated on the chocolate—some were licking the walls, others were **DIVING** into the fountain.

"Don't worry, gentlemen!" Willy called up to them. "You'll come down eventually, *I think*. Until then, we need to figure out what to do with this chocolate." He dipped his finger into the fountain and gave it a taste. He shuddered. "Now, some say good chocolate should be simple, plain, uncomplicated . . ." He began pulling bottles out of his pocket and chucking them in the fountain. "But I like a little complication, elaboration, and innovation—in short, WONKAFICATION."

Suddenly, the chocolate in the fountain began to bubble and turned a GLORIOUS shade of purple.

"Ladies and gentlemen," Willy said grandly, "my friends and I invite you to enjoy our chocolate!"

The workers rushed to his side, and together they watched as the Cartel grew smaller and smaller in the sky, a squabbling mass of men **RISING** up and up, before disappearing from sight.

CHAPTER TWENTY-EIGHT

ARREST THEM

Back at the washhouse, Mrs. Scrubitt was organizing the bundles of money into piles and labeling them.

"Nice old house in the country," she said, tapping one pile. "Massive barrel of worm water, fancy new pants—"

But she was interrupted by Bleacher, who **BURST** in and bolted the door hastily behind him.

"It's the Cartel!" he hissed. "They've gone down!"

Mrs. Scrubitt rose **QUICKLY** to her feet. "Well . . . we didn't do nothin'! Except poison all those chocolates!"

There was a knock at the door.

"Police!" came a shout, followed by more knocking.

"Quick!" Mrs. Scrubitt cried. "Eat the evidence!"

"Police!"

"Just a second, officer!" Mrs. Scrubitt cried. "I'm on the toilet . . ."

They grabbed the tray of strange bottles they'd stolen from Willy and began gulping down what remained inside them.

"Almost done, officer!" Mrs. Scrubitt shouted. "Oh no, still more toileting to go!"

"Scrubitt, Bleacher, OPEN UP or we will knock this door down!"

And they did knock it down. But when the poor arresting officers burst in, they found not so much two criminals but instead two massive mounds of hair with eyes. Mrs. Scrubitt had long blue hair to her ankles and a matching blue beard, and Bleacher had green hair, which he pulled back off his swollen face to reveal some yellow-spotted skin.

It took a while, but the officers eventually found their arms and put them in handcuffs. As they did so, Mrs. Scrubitt struggled free and oozed, "One last kiss, my lord, before we are forever parted?"

"Oh, **PUFFY-WUFF**!" Bleacher said, and they kissed, one final, slobbery, wormy kiss.

CHAPTER TWENTY-NINE

DREAMS AND PROMISES

Willy sat on the steps of the cathedral, watching the whole city enjoy the rich chocolate flowing from the fountain. He felt a **WARMTH** wrapping around him. It was a feeling he hadn't felt since he was a small boy on a small boat . . .

He reached into his pocket and pulled out his old birthday bar of chocolate.

Finally, it was time.

He took a deep breath and peeled back the wrapper. But much to his surprise, there came a brilliant flash of GOLD!

Willy's heart stood still. Slowly, he removed the rest of the wrapper and held the gold paper up to the light. There was a faint message on it. A message that now—thanks to Noodle—he could read.

The secret is . . . it's not the chocolate that matters. It's the people you share it with!

Love,

Mama

Willy traced her words with his finger, tears wetting his cheeks. He could feel eyes on him, like she was there. He looked up hopefully—and there she was. Standing in the crowd, looking back at him.

"You kept your word," he whispered. "You're here, Mama."

She smiled proudly at him and then gestured at

the chocolate in his hand. Willy raised it in the air with a lump in his throat. He knew it would be the very last chocolate of hers that he would ever eat, and as the tears fell, he snapped off the corner and popped it in his mouth.

His mother clasped her hands with **JOY**, just as she had done on every birthday, every time they'd shared chocolate together before. He wanted to cry out, to grab hold of her and keep her forever, but he knew he couldn't. As the chocolate melted in his mouth, she began to fade, softer and softer, fainter and fainter, and then she was gone. But she would never truly be gone, not really. He knew that now.

Noodle came skipping toward him, and Willy wiped his tears and broke off a piece of chocolate for her. As she chewed on it, a look of pure joy spread across her face.

One by one, the rest of the washhouse workers

joined them, and he handed them each a piece of chocolate. They ate the whole bar together, all of them like one big family.

It was just as he had dreamed. No—it was even better than that.

"This really is the best chocolate," Noodle said.

Willy smiled at the empty wrapper in his hand. "I wish it could last **FOREVER**."

The cathedral bells chimed.

"I guess it's time," Willy said.

"Time for what?" Noodle asked. "What's going on?"

The other workers began grinning and nudging each other excitedly.

"You know how many people called D. Smith live in this city, Noodle?" Willy asked.

"One hundred and six," Abacus answered. "We checked in the phone book."

"But luckily," Willy said, "you have a friend

who works at the telephone exchange, and she spent the whole afternoon ringing around—and guess what!"

"We **FOUND** her!" Lottie squeaked.

Noodle froze in shock. "You found my mom? You found Dorothy Smith?"

"None of us felt right going home until you had a home too," Abacus said.

Willy held out his arm. "Come on, Noodle. I think you're going to like where we're going."

CHAPTER THIRTY

Z

"The library?" Noodle gasped. "My mom works at the library?"

"And lives here, too," Willy said. "In a house of **IMAGINATION**! Isn't it wonderful?! It's just like you dreamed. A beautiful old building full of books."

The place was very grand, with windows that shone with welcoming light. And it was tall, too. It needed to be, because inside it housed more characters, more cities, and more creatures than even Willy had met on his travels. And though many thought of it as a quiet place, really, there was nowhere in the world more full of life and loudness.

Noodle opened her mouth to speak, but no words came out. On the steps stood a woman, waiting patiently—like she had been waiting there forever. She was tall, like the library itself, and sunbeams bounced off the snow beneath her feet, lighting her up like an **ANGEL**.

"Off you go, now," Willy said, and he gently nudged her toward the steps.

Noodle climbed the stairs, slowly at first, then faster and faster. Willy watched with joy as Noodle's mother pulled her into a hug that looked like it would never end. Noodle peeked out at Willy and mouthed, "Thank you."

He smiled and gathered his cane. It was time to go.

But just as he turned to leave, a voice made him stop dead in his tracks.

"So goes a good deed in a weary world."

Willy looked down to see the Oompa-Loompa at his feet.

"I wondered if I'd see you again," Willy said. "Thank you for saving my life in the vault." He rummaged around in his case and produced a fresh jar of chocolates.

"I suppose that concludes our business," the Oompa-Loompa said, grabbing them. "I shall now return to my beloved **LOOMPALAND**, where cacao beans grow in disappointingly small numbers and my friends look down on me."

"I thought they called you Lofty?" Willy said.

The Oompa-Loompa shifted awkwardly. "As a matter of fact, I am a quarter inch below average. They call me Shorty-Pants. Still, good day, sir."

Willy frowned. "Oh, it's a shame you have to go."

The Oompa-Loompa turned and began marching off. "I said good day."

"If I'm going to share my chocolate with the world, I need more than a shop. I need a factory . . ."

"Yes, well, good luck with that," the Oompa-Loompa said.

"And someone to head up the tasting department."

The Oompa-Loompa ground to a halt and **SWIVELED** on his heel to face Willy.

"I suppose I don't have to rush back," he said. "Tell me more about this factory."

"Well, for starters, it'll need to be **BIG**," Willy said as the pair walked off down the road together. "And it *must* have a chocolate river . . ."

EPILOGUE

WONKA

Noodle was so very happy in her new home in the library with a kindhearted mother and a never-ending reading pile. Though it had only been months, she felt as if she had been there her whole life. The horrible years at Scrubitt and Bleacher had already begun to fade, worn thin in her memory by every warm **HUG** from her mother.

Life had become predictable and ordinary and truly wonderful, though her friend Willy had MYSTERIOUSLY disappeared. No one knew where he had gone, and everyone missed his chocolates.

But one night, after she slipped a bookmark into her book and went to the bathroom to brush her teeth, she found a note tacked to the sink.

Dear Noodle,

I once promised you a lifetime supply of chocolate, and Willy Wonka always keeps his word. In your house you've got hot and cold running water, of course. But I changed it. You now have "hot" and "chocolate." My chocolate.

She twisted the tap and gasped as rich, melted chocolate gushed out of it!

Whenever you drink it, I hope you'll think of me. I know I'll be thinking of you.

Your friend,
Willy Wonka

PS: If you ever need to get in touch, simply ask the little orange man with the green hair.

"Little orange man with green hair," she said with a tut. But then she spotted something on the floor. She crouched down, her hands tracing the **IMPOSSIBLE** outline of—

"Tiny footprints!" she cried.

Quickly, she followed them back into her bedroom, around the drawers, along the bookcase, under the bed, and all the way to the window . . . where a very small man was standing on the ledge!

An orange man with green hair.

She stood frozen in shock before giving a small, shy wave. He offered her a slight nod in formal acknowledgment in return.

She couldn't believe it. He was real all along.

Then quite suddenly he burst to life, pulling strings at his side. There was a great *clunk*, and mechanical wings unfurled from his jacket—and he jumped right out of the window!

Noodle rushed over and watched with utter joy as the Oompa-Loompa dipped low, skimming the cobbles, then swooped up and soared off into the night.

He flew up high past the silhouette of a factory, and as he glided over it, the sign on the roof burst to life in lights. Just one word, more delicious than moonlight: